A PLACE BETWEEN

A PLACE BETWEEN

A NOVEL BY
SUZANNE NEWTON

VIKING KESTREL

VIKING KESTREL
Viking Penguin Inc., 40 West 23rd Street, New York, New York 10010, U.S.A.
Penguin Books Ltd, Harmondsworth, Middlesex, England
Penguin Books Australia Ltd, Ringwood, Victoria, Australia
Penguin Books Canada Limited, 2801 John Street, Markham, Ontario, Canada L3R 1B4
Penguin Books (N.Z.) Ltd, 182–190 Wairau Road, Auckland 10, New Zealand

First published in 1986 by Viking Penguin Inc.
Published simultaneously in Canada
Printed in U.S.A. by The Book Press, Brattleboro, Vermont
Set in Electra
1 2 3 4 5 90 89 88 87 86

Library of Congress Cataloging in Publication Data
Newton, Suzanne.   A place between.
Summary: Arden must move from her beloved hometown to an unwelcoming
city and adjust to living with her widowed grandmother.
[1. Moving, Household—Fiction.   2. Grandmothers—
Fiction]   I. Title.
PZ7.M4875P1   1986   [Fic]   86-5520   ISBN 0-670-80778-8

For Jay,
Hannis III,
and Patsy

A PLACE BETWEEN

CHAPTER ONE

USUALLY, COMING HOME AFTER A WEEK AT THE RIVER WAS Arden Gifford's most unfavorite part of the summer vacation. Everything had to be unloaded from the car and put away. Dirty clothes and linens had to be sorted and washed. Someone had to make a trip to the store for enough bread and milk for Monday's breakfast. This time, though, as she climbed the stairs with her suitcase, she still basked in the glow of Big Dad's praise for the seven fish she had caught yesterday. Thanks to her, the whole family had enjoyed a delicious fish dinner on their last night together at the cottage. She couldn't wait to tell her friends, DorJo and Seth.

Arden wrinkled her nose at the musty smell of a house closed for seven days. At the door to her room, she put down her burden and crossed to open a window, pausing a moment to look out at the great oaks spreading cool shade over the back-yard. Haverlee really was a good place to come home to, even at the end of a muggy July day.

The telephone rang and she raced downstairs to answer it. Mr. Briggs, Dad's boss at the EZ Life Appliances plant, was on the line.

"Just a minute, Mr. Briggs. Dad's coming in right now with a load of baggage from our trip."

Dad made a face at her as she held out the receiver. "Hold it for me, Bird," he said in a low voice. "I don't want to put this stuff down until I get it to where it belongs."

She held the receiver to his ear, watching his eyes as he listened. She wasn't particularly interested in the conversation. Plant talk was boring, all about production and output and down time.

"Well, I suppose I could," Dad said reluctantly. "Could you give me half an hour? We just got back—"

He listened some more. "All right. I'll get there as soon as I can. Sure. 'Bye." He nodded to Arden to put the receiver back in its cradle. She heard the click as Mr. Briggs hung up. Dad had a funny expression on his face.

"What's the matter?" she asked. "Did the plant blow up while you were away?"

"No." Ignoring her little joke, he headed toward the kitchen with a full laundry bag under one arm and a box of groceries under the other. "Arden, there are some more boxes in the car," he called back over his shoulder. "Get them out, will you?"

Feeling a bit slighted, she wandered out to the car, taking her time, looking up and down the street in hopes that Seth or DorJo might happen by, but it wasn't the right time of day for that. More than anything else, she wanted to go over to DorJo's and compare weeks—DorJo had gone away to camp for the first time ever—but it wouldn't be fair to leave Mom, Hill, and Dad with all the work to do.

"Hey, Aardvark!" Hill said, bursting out of the house. "Hurry up, will you? Dad wants the car emptied right now."

"Something's happened at the plant, hasn't it?" she asked, as he passed her.

"I don't know. Dad doesn't look too happy." Hill grabbed the heaviest box, leaving her a smaller one and a sleeping bag. She watched him go back inside, thinking how tall and muscular he had become. Last winter and spring, he had lived with Gran and Big Dad in Grierson so that he could attend Pressley High School. He would be going back there in September for his senior year. Yesterday, while she and Big Dad fished, she had tried to explain to him how Hill didn't seem at home in Haverlee anymore.

"Well," Big Dad had said, "I expect he feels like he doesn't really have a place of his own, for all he's welcome at our home and yours. He's wilderness wandering."

"What do you mean, wilderness wandering?"

"You remember the Israelites, how they left Egypt and wandered around in the wilderness for forty years before they could enter the Promised Land? And before that, Abraham—he left his home in Ur and 'went out he knew not where.' And Elijah and Jesus?"

"Yes, but how is that like Hill?"

"We all have times when we leave one place but we don't go right straight to another one," Big Dad had said. With his glasses on the middle of his nose and the old gray felt fishing hat pulled low over his forehead, he looked very wise. "We kind of end up in a between place, like between third base and home, with the catcher eyeing us from one direction and the third baseman from the other. The scary part is knowing that you can't go back to where you came from."

Big Dad had said that everyone had such wandering times. Well, *she* certainly didn't intend to! It was Hill's own fault for choosing to leave Haverlee, she thought as she picked up her bundles and closed the car trunk. She was quite happy to stay in Haverlee forever.

Dad came out just as she got to the front door. "'Bye, Bird," he said, giving her a hasty peck on the cheek as he swept past. "See you after a while."

He was gone before she could ask him anything. Putting the box and sleeping bag in the hall, she went straight to the kitchen, where Mom was taking cans and jars of food out of the box Dad had brought in.

"Arden, do you feel like walking to the store? I know it's hot, but we have to have bread and milk."

"Sure." She began helping Mom take items from the box, grouping them on the shelves where they belonged. "What's the matter at the plant?"

"I don't know." Mom's tone indicated that she didn't want to talk about it. "Here—get some money out of my wallet and go to the store. I'll finish putting things away."

Arden did as she was told, picking a ten from among the ones and fives in the red leather wallet. She liked the smell of Mom's wallet, a mixture of leather and something sweet like face powder.

"May DorJo go with me?"

"As long as you don't dawdle." The short answers were very unlike Mom. "Be back in forty minutes. Milk and bread is all I need for now, but you and DorJo may have an ice cream sandwich if you like."

Arden checked her Timex and wound it, making sure it showed the same time as the rooster clock over the refrigerator. "I'll be back in forty minutes flat," she said as she went out.

To make more time for talking, she ran most of the way to DorJo's. She found her friend sitting on the side porch, munching an apple. When she caught sight of Arden, she leaped to her feet and ran to meet her.

6

"I've been home since yesterday," she said as they hugged each other. "When did you get back?"

"About twenty minutes ago. I have to run to the store for Mom. Can you go with me? We could talk on the way. I can't wait to hear about camp."

At that moment, DorJo's mother came to the screen door. Mrs. Huggins had lost a lot of weight since last year. Her clothes didn't fit very well, but her hair was neatly combed. She was really a pretty good-looking woman, Arden thought, now that she took care of herself. These day she had a steady job at a nursing home, and she never left home for parts unknown the way she used to.

"Hey, Arden," she said. Although her manner was still brusque and startling, it no longer bothered Arden. She had gotten used to it.

"Hello, Mrs. Huggins. May DorJo walk with me to the store?"

"I suppose. But don't y'all stay gone all evenin', y'hear?"

"Yes, ma'am," Arden said politely. Mrs. Huggins knew perfectly well that they would be right back, but she liked to have the feeling that she was being obeyed. That was okay with Arden, so long as she and DorJo had time to talk.

They started to the store with arms linked, but it was hard for them to keep in step. DorJo's five feet eight and long legs were too much of a contrast to Arden's barely five feet, one inch. Soon they gave it up and just walked side by side. DorJo's black hair was much shorter now, cut close to her head and sort of fluffy on top. Her older sister, Jessie, who was going to beauty school in Porterfield, had given her the haircut just before DorJo left for camp. Arden thought it made DorJo look very grownup and pretty, but she was careful not to say so. DorJo had never wanted to be either one of those things.

"Well, tell me about camp," Arden said. "Everything."

"It was real fine," DorJo said. "I don't think I ever had so much fun in my whole life!"

Arden experienced a sudden and unexpected stab of envy, which she quickly put down. After all, it was pretty wonderful for DorJo to be able to go to camp. Mom had managed to get the camp scholarship for her with the help of the minister of their church.

"Well, don't stop," she said. "*Tell* me."

"There were people from everywhere in the state," said DorJo. "Most of them knew each other from going to camp before, but that didn't keep them from treating me like one of them . . . friendly and all. They'd come up and talk like they'd known me forever."

Arden smiled. DorJo had always been a person to herself, guarded in her friendships.

"The thing is, by the second day *I* started doing it—going up to strangers and talking, I mean. We had gatherings around the campfire in the evening, and we had worship in the morning before breakfast . . . " Her voice trailed off. She seemed transported back to the previous week. "The truth is," she added after a moment, "I'm homesick for that place. I hated to leave. I didn't know if I could stand to come back."

"Well, at least you can go there again next year," Arden said.

"Oh, I will!" DorJo spoke with conviction. "I wouldn't miss it for anything. I'm going to get a job and save my money."

Arden laughed. "Remember what a time I had persuading you to go? You thought of a hundred reasons why you shouldn't."

"I'm glad you didn't let me get out of it." DorJo looked sheepish. "I hope *you* can go next year. Everytime we did something fun, I'd wish you were there."

"Maybe it's a good thing I wasn't," Arden said. "You might not have made so many new friends."

"I'm going to write to a couple of them," DorJo said.

They were almost to the store by that time. Arden glanced at her Timex, to be sure they weren't dawdling. "Who?" she asked, as she pushed open the door and they entered the air-conditioned atmosphere.

"Bitsy Kirk is one. She lives in Winston-Salem."

Arden picked up a loaf of bread from one of the shelves and headed toward the refrigerated cabinet where the dairy products were kept. "Who else?" She opened the cabinet to reach for the gallon of milk. She thought, as she hefted it, how hard it was going to be to lug home the heavy milk carton and a soft loaf of bread while trying to eat a fast-melting ice cream sandwich.

DorJo, instead of answering, turned away from Arden to the cabinet where ice cream was kept. She made herself very busy scrounging among the merchandise for ice cream sandwiches that didn't show signs of previous thawing.

"His name's Mark Burns," she mumbled.

"You mean, a *boy*?" Arden's astonishment banished all tact. It was about the last thing in the world she expected to hear from DorJo.

"Shhh!" DorJo looked around hastily as though fearful someone would overhear. Her complexion was pink.

Arden felt that the space between them had suddenly widened and lengthened. She didn't know what to say. Neither did DorJo. They carried the items to the checkout counter and stood silently while the checker gave Arden change and handed her the sack of groceries. The girls went out into the warm, damp afternoon without looking at each other.

"Maybe if you could hold the loaf of bread it wouldn't get smushed," Arden suggested. They stopped under a tree to unwrap their ice cream and divide the load between them, then they started on their way again.

9

"Well, tell me about Bitsy and Mark." Arden was careful to include both names, so as not to place more importance on the boy than on the girl.

"I don't know what to tell," DorJo said miserably. She licked the ice cream around the edge of the chocolate cookie. "I like 'em both a lot. Bitsy is about my height and has red hair and green eyes. I never saw anybody with eyes so green. And she's the kind of person everybody likes because she's friendly. I couldn't believe she picked me out to be special friends, but it was like we had known each other since day one."

Arden's stomach felt tight. She reminded herself that Bitsy was in Winston-Salem and that DorJo probably wouldn't see her again until next year.

"And how about Mark?" she asked.

DorJo bit the sandwich and made the ice cream squish out around the edges. She made much of licking the squished cream before she answered. "He's something!" she said softly. "He's taller than me and he's in the eleventh grade. He was a camp counselor."

"Eleventh grade!" Arden was shocked. "Gosh, DorJo—he must be seventeen years old!"

"Sixteen," DorJo said promptly. "He won't be seventeen until October."

As if that made any difference. Of course, DorJo was almost fourteen herself, being one of the older students in their class.

"Did he . . . does he like you?"

DorJo ate the rest of the sandwich in one large bite. The mouthful kept her from answering for half a minute, but then she had to respond.

"Bitsy and me talked about it," she said at last. "She liked him, too. We were trying to figure out which of us he liked best." She sighed. "It's prob'ly her. She's too pretty and friendly not to win."

10

Arden felt a rush of real sympathy for her friend, and a twinge of irritation at this Mark Burns, who probably had a steady girlfriend back in—wherever he came from.

"I wasn't going to tell you this, DorJo," she said, "because I thought it would make you mad. But ever since Jessie gave you that haircut, you've been about the best-looking person I know. So if you think that Bitsy person is prettier than you, she has to be Miss America or something."

It was DorJo's turn to be astonished. She stopped in her tracks and stared at Arden, her mouth open as though she couldn't breathe very well. "Do you mean that?"

"Yes. You know I wouldn't tell you a lie."

DorJo began walking again, like someone in a trance. She swung the loaf of bread by the bag opening, back and forth like a pendulum. Arden had never seen her like this—sort of our of her mind.

"I don't want you to tell a soul about this," DorJo said suddenly. "You're the only person in this town who knows. I'm not telling Mama or Granpa, or even Jessie."

Arden felt burdened with an unwelcome weight. Did this mean she would have to hear all about Mark Burns every time she and DorJo got together? The prospect made her glum. "Okay," she said. "I promise."

DorJo gave her a grateful look. "I don't know what I'd do if you weren't here. Bust, I guess!"

"Well, I certainly wouldn't want you to do *that*," Arden said; "it's so messy."

DorJo laughed, more from relief maybe than because what Arden said was funny. They had reached DorJo's house by this time and she handed over the loaf of bread. "Thanks for coming by for me—I'll see you tomorrow sometime."

Arden turned away and headed toward home. The sun was behind the houses now and long shadows cooled the street. What a strange homecoming this was! Arden felt pushed toward a place where she did not want to go. Just thinking about it made her slow her steps and set her jaw in protest.

CHAPTER TWO

ARDEN PUT THE GALLON OF MILK AND THE LOAF OF BREAD INTO the refrigerator. She had a cold spot in the crook of her left arm from cradling the milk for so long.

"Thanks for doing that, Arden." Mom seemed distracted. "We'll have supper in about thirty minutes."

"Any word from Dad?" Arden ventured.

Mom shook her head.

"Are you worried?"

Mom looked directly at Arden and exhaled, as though the energy had gone out of her. "Yes."

The word slit the air, leaving a hole like a tear in a sack. Things were about to spill through. Feeling a little sick, Arden said, "I'll wash my hands and set the table. Back in a minute."

In the bathroom, she looked at herself in the mirror, slightly amazed that she didn't look pale and frightened. When Mom got worried, things were serious. She washed her hands quickly, then went back to the kitchen. She set the table and did other chores for Mom, very aware of the silence between them. Finally Mom told her to call Hill to supper.

Arden wished she knew what was to be feared, but for the life of her she couldn't imagine. Dad had worked at EZ Life Appliances since before she was born. He was second man from the top, in line for the manager's position. Maybe the plant *did* burn down while they were gone, despite what Dad had said. Or perhaps there was a burglary and a lot of equipment was stolen. Maybe—

Hill was coming out of his room as she reached the top of the stairs.

"Supper's ready," she said. "Mom's upset."

She realized as soon as she spoke that the two phrases didn't go together. Hill's laughter echoed in the hall. Other times, she would have joined him, but now she was offended. Things were too serious for laughter. "I mean it," she said, not smiling. "Something's the matter."

Hill sobered instantly. "What is it?"

"I don't know." She lowered her voice to a whisper. "It's something about Dad and the plant. I think it's serious."

"Why do you say that?"

"Mom always looks on the bright side of things," Arden said. "But she's acting like she's . . . I don't know!"

"Hmmm. Must be something that's been brewing for a while." Hill stuck his hands in his pockets as they went downstairs.

Ah, that was it! Mom knew something that she and Hill did not. It wasn't just today's phone call. The enlightenment brought Arden relief only for an instant, though. If something had been brewing, then Dad and Mom had been keeping it a secret for no telling how long.

When she and Hill came into the kitchen, Mom was already seated at her place. Her shoulders slumped, and she rested her head in her hands. Arden went straight to her and put an arm around her shoulders. Mom leaned against her briefly.

"Thanks," she said. "Sorry I'm such a blob. Getting back from the river wears me out."

Hill sat down opposite her. "It's not just that, is it, Mom?" Arden kept standing where she was, with her arm across Mom's shoulders, watching Hill's eyes as though they were a mirror to reflect what Mom was thinking.

"Well, no," Mom said. "But it takes a lot out of me, so that . . . other things are harder to handle."

"What things?" Hill's questions were like hammer beats. Arden moved away from Mom and sat down at her place.

"You ask too many questions," said Mom. "Say the blessing."

Hill obeyed, but as soon as he said amen, he raised his head and said, "I think you ought to tell us."

"I don't know what to tell," Mom answered, looking from one to the other.

"Well, you can tell us what's been going on," Arden spoke up. "When Dad comes home, it might help for us to know something, so we won't ask him a lot of dumb questions."

Mom gave her a long look and then nodded. "Maybe you're right. I'll tell you what I can."

It seemed that EZ Life Appliances had fallen on hard times. The larger manufacturers of small appliances could offer rebates and other incentives to get their customers to buy, but EZ Life could not. Plant costs had been going up steadily and profits were declining. The Board had already warned Dad and Mr. Briggs several months before that if they didn't pull out of the slump, the Haverlee plant would have to close.

"What I fear," Mom said finally, "is that sometime during this past week the Board may have made that decision."

Arden stared at Mom, trying to take in what she had heard. "But . . . what will Dad do?"

"I don't know. And of course I may be wrong. If I am, I hate to have upset the two of you for no reason."

Hill didn't say anything right away. He bit off a large hunk of sandwich and chewed with great concentration. Finally, he swallowed and said, "EZ Life has a plant in Grierson. Is that going to close, too?"

"Probably not," Mom said. "They were thinking of consolidating the Haverlee and Grierson operations. They only built here to begin with because labor costs were lower."

"Dad can get another job here—I just know he can," Arden said in a thin voice. "Everybody likes him."

"Well, you know your dad wouldn't want just any job," Mom said. "He would want something that uses his skills and experience, and that pays as well as this one. Haverlee doesn't have many of those kinds of jobs, Arden."

Arden took a small bite of sandwich, but her mouth was so dry she couldn't chew it up. The question she dared not ask was, Do we have to move? She had never known such panic as now washed over her.

"Maybe we're making a mountain out of a molehill," she managed to say.

Mom reached over and took her hand. "Arden, it's all a big question mark."

"Yes'm." Arden's throat felt tight. "I think I'd like to be excused from the table for a few minutes."

Upstairs in her room, she stood in the middle of the floor hugging herself. It couldn't be true. Things didn't change this fast. When Dad got home, he would reassure them that all their worries were for nothing.

Then why was she so frightened?

She went over to the window seat and curled up on it,

16

gazing out the window at the yard shaded by great oaks. What if they had to move from Haverlee? What if, by next year this time, she could no longer sit here and look out this window? The thought was scary.

Her thoughts flew back to last evening when they had all sat on the screened porch at the river cottage, watching quiet points of light flash first from the fireflies in the yard and then, as though in response, from the buoys out in the river. Gran and Big Dad were in the porch swing. Arden's chair was between Mom's and Dad's. She had been close enough to touch them both. Hill's tall silhouette, dark against the moonlight, had stood a little apart from the rest.

"I don't want this summer to be over," she had said.

"I know," said Mom. "It's a shame we can't stretch good times so they'll last longer."

"The older you get, the faster time flies," Gran said, moving closer to Big Dad.

"Well," he had said, "this is what we've got, so don't worry yourself about tomorrow or next week. Here we are, right now. Let's be thankful for it."

A moment of chastened silence had followed his words, then Gran began singing, "There's a long, long trail a-winding, into the land of my dreams . . . " Big Dad joined in with his deep bass, Mom with the alto, and Hill and Dad struggled with the tenor part. Arden sang the melody along with Gran. She knew lots of old songs from listening to her parents and grandparents sing. Last night the music's strong chords were calming, but now the memory made her sad.

When she heard Dad's car coming along the street she was caught between wanting to race downstairs and wanting to hide in the closet. She chose, finally, to go down slowly, back to the kitchen where Mom and Hill were. Her scarcely touched sandwich still lay on the plate. The sight of it made her ill.

"Are you all right, Arden?" Mom pulled her close.

"Scared," she muttered.

Mom didn't say, "Oh, there's nothing to be scared of," or any of those kinds of words, just gave her a squeeze and a pat and let her go.

When Dad walked in, she knew right away that the worst had happened. He looked exhausted. His eyes met Mom's and seemed to say, This Is It.

He washed his hands at the sink and dried them, then sat down—all without saying a word. Mom got up and put her arms around his shoulders.

"Have you told them?" he asked, as though Arden and Hill weren't even sitting there.

"Yes. I told them what might happen."

Dad looked at Hill, who was sitting straight in the chair as though he might leap to his feet at any moment. Then he looked at Arden, who felt that she had turned into a piece of wood, immovable and dark. She stared back at him so intently her eyes burned.

"Well." He sighed, turning his hands palm up on the table. "The recession has reached Haverlee." He glanced up at Mom. "Kind of like the polio epidemics, Joan—or the Black Plague."

Mom patted his shoulder and sat down again. "What's the verdict—in terms of time, I mean?"

"December. We'll shut down gradually—still have some orders to fill, but we won't be taking new orders from now on."

December. Arden counted on her fingers out of sight under the table. All of August, September, October, November. Part of December. Would they spend Christmas here? Would Dad even consider not leaving Haverlee?

"I'm sorry, kids," Dad said to Hill and Arden. "We tried."

18

"It's not your fault, Dad," Hill said. "It's happening everywhere—even the big companies."

"I know, but that doesn't make it any easier. It feels like failure. I can't help thinking that we could've pulled it off, with a little luck." Arden thought of a piece of flower stem cut too near the bloom. No hope, no second chances.

Dad was still talking. "On my way home, I was thinking about what's next."

"You don't have to deal with that right now," Mom said firmly. "Eat something. Tomorrow's soon enough to think about what's next."

Dad picked up his sandwich. "I'd be happy to hear any suggestions anyone might have," he said, just before taking a bite.

Arden started to speak, but Mom intervened. "We'll all have our ideas at the right time. We won't do anything but scare ourselves if we talk about it right now. Maybe we can have a family meeting tomorrow night at dinner, after we've had a chance to think."

Dad actually smiled. He reached over and squeezed Mom's hand. "I knew I married you for some good reason," he said.

Mom pretended to be insulted. "Well, I thought I'd *never* get a chance to show my stuff!"

Hill laughed outright. Arden grinned in spite of the lump in her throat. They all began to eat. Perhaps the stem was not too short after all.

CHAPTER THREE

THE HUMID AUGUST DAYS PASSED TOO RAPIDLY. ARDEN WAS convinced it was because they might have to move.

"It seems strange, having to overhaul this résumé," Dad said one evening, looking through a sheaf of papers on his desk. "When I got the job at EZ Life, I thought I'd never have to look for another."

"You should start sending copies out right away," Mom advised. "It takes time to get replies."

Dad sat down in his big brown leather chair and stared into space for a while; then he said, "I think I'm going to take some time off to go to Grierson. Maybe I'll go next Sunday and stay until Tuesday evening. That would give me two days to check with some employment agencies and look at the Grierson plant to see whether I should even entertain any hopes." He looked around the room at them. "Anyone want to go along?"

"I can't," said Mom. "I'd better work as much as I can, so we won't have our backs to the wall come December."

"I'm sorry, Joan." Dad looked apologetic.

"Don't worry about it," she said. "If I lost my job while *you* were working, I wouldn't exactly expect you to throw me out on the street because I couldn't do my part."

"I can't go either," said Hill. "Two people are taking vacations next week and I have to fill their shifts. I'll be moving back to Grierson at the end of the month, anyway. I guess I'll wait till then."

Dad looked at Arden, who was pretending to read, although she was listening to every word. "Knowing how you feel about Grierson, I suppose your going is out of the question."

"Maybe I will, though," she said, surprising herself more than anyone.

Dad brightened. "I'd be glad for your company. Gran and Big Dad would like it, too. It's been a long time since you went to visit them without the rest of the family along. We'd be back Tuesday night, so you'd be here for your birthday on Friday."

"Well, I'll go. Only, I hope Gran won't invite those stuck-up town girls over. Tell her I have plans."

Mom's eyebrows went up. "Oh? What plans?"

"I'll think of something," Arden answered, ducking behind her book again.

When she and Dad left for Grierson, Arden was in good spirits. In some ways, it was like the old days when she was Gran's and Big Dad's special guest for a whole week once each year. Those had been good times, she had to admit. She fell to wondering why her attitude had changed, and when.

She was the only granddaughter—Uncle Bob had two sons—and she could remember that Gran always seemed very happy to have her because of all the girl toys she had saved from her childhood for someone to play with. The lovely china tea set that Gran's big brother had brought from England after World War I, the dolls and doll clothes—all of these had made Arden look forward to the week in Grierson.

But for the past year or so she had the feeling that Gran wasn't satisfied with her. She wasn't doing or being something that Gran wanted. Several times, on short family visits, Arden had almost asked what the matter was, but she couldn't quite bring herself to do it. Gran might tell her, and then she'd have to change—or at least that was how it felt.

"I'm glad you decided to come with me, Bird," Dad said as they drove along. "Keeps me from being lonesome."

"Are you just saying that?" Arden asked.

"You know me better than that. I've missed our talking times. I've been thinking how hard all this change is for you. I know how you feel about Haverlee."

She got an unexpected lump in her throat. Dad shouldn't be sympathetic. It pushed her sorry-for-myself button.

"The rest of us can be more philosophical," Dad went on, "at least about moving. You're the one who cares most about our staying where we are."

She stared straight ahead, watching the landscape divide before them and whiz by on either side. "It's three against one. It wouldn't be right for one person to keep the whole family from doing something."

"But every person in the family is important," Dad said. "Hill moved to Grierson last year because that's what he wanted most. The rest of us hated to see him go, but it was still the best thing for him."

"Then would you let me stay in Haverlee . . . with DorJo?" she asked in a rush of words. "Even if the rest of you moved away?"

Dad didn't reply immediately. He took one hand from the steering wheel and smoothed back his hair. "That's hard, Bird," he said at last. "You don't have relatives in Haverlee. I don't think we would have let Hill leave if he hadn't been moving in with Gran and Big Dad. Also, although Haverlee is a place to love, it's not really a place to grow—"

"That's not true!" she interrupted. "That is absolutely not true!"

"Now, hold on," Dad said gently. "Let me finish. You're every bit as bright as Hill, but your intellect won't be stretched in Haverlee."

"I don't want it stretched," she grumped. "Why does everybody think being the smartest is so important? I'm satisfied. Everybody doesn't have to be the world's genius!"

"Sure—you're right. But I'm thinking that there may be some talent or interest that you haven't discovered yet, and you won't in Haverlee because there's nothing there to bring it out."

She folded her arms tightly across her chest, thinking that the trip to Grierson with Dad was not such a hot idea after all. Well, he could talk till Doomsday. She would never change her mind. What kind of person did he think she was anyhow, that she would so easily give up everything that was dear to her?

Dad didn't try to argue anymore. During the rest of the trip, they talked mostly about how he would go about finding a new job. Arden hadn't realized how complicated the process was, or how scary.

"I'll tell you what it feels like, Bird," said Dad. "Imagine that you've lived inside a cozy, well-furnished house built to last forever, and then all of a sudden you wake up one morning and find out that the house has disappeared from around you. You're lying there in a bed right out in the open—no walls, no ceiling. Just—"

"Wilderness," Arden said without thinking. The picture she

23

had in mind was of a bed in the middle of a desert. She thought about the talk that she and Big Dad had had about wilderness wandering.

"Yes," he said, giving her an odd look. "Yes, it is kind of like that."

"Well, wilderness wandering is only temporary. Big Dad said so. I think it won't be long before you get your house back."

"I hope you're right," he said. They passed the sign at the Grierson city limits. "But it may not be exactly the same house. I may not even want it to be. I might settle for a tent."

She laughed at that. "Why?"

"They're portable. And if they get blown down, they're not that hard to set up again."

"But they also make it easier to move around," she said. "You might end up moving every year. If you do, don't expect *me* to go along."

It was Dad's turn to laugh. "Don't forget, we're not talking about a *real* tent, Bird."

The house in Grierson was cool and inviting and smelled like the beef that was roasting in the oven. After hugs from Gran and Big Dad and the hauling in of suitcases, the four of them settled in chairs on the back porch with glasses of iced lemonade.

"Well, Tom," Gran said with a little explosion of breath, as though she had been holding the words longer than she could stand. "Tell us what kind of progress you're making in your job-hunting."

"Now, Sally—" Big Dad began.

"Now, Sally, nothing!" Gran cut him off. "We might as well talk about it and clear the air, Jake. I want to know what's happening, whether you do or not."

"Whether I want to know has nothing to do with it!" Big Dad said testily. "Think of Tom's feelings."

24

They argued as though Dad were not even there. Arden looked at him with questions in her eyes. He winked at her, shrugging his shoulders ever so slightly.

Gran must have seen it, because she turned to him and said, "All right, are you going to tell us or not?"

"What do you want to know?" Dad asked, trying to look properly serious.

Gran spread her fingers. "Anything. All we know is that your plant is closing in December."

"Yes," said Big Dad, "and Sally wants to know if we're going to have to spend our retirement savings on you while you look for other work."

"Jake!"

"I don't think you'll need to worry about that," Dad said. "We're okay. Joan's working and we have a pretty good nest egg to fall back on."

"So you don't really know what your next employment will be, then?" Gran said.

Dad shook his head. "That's why I came to Grierson. I need to do some serious looking. There's the possibility of an opening in the Grierson plant, but I can't count on it."

"I do so wish you'd come back here," Gran said wistfully. "I've always thought that you and Joan shouldn't have stuck yourselves way off down there in Haverlee."

Arden clamped her teeth together to keep from saying something rude. She definitely did not like Gran's attitude toward Haverlee.

"Haverlee has been a good place for the kids to grow up," Dad said.

"Well, I certainly hope you don't intend to stay there at all costs," Gran said.

"Sally, you are going too far." Big Dad spoke with great firmness. Gran pressed her lips together and stopped arguing.

"It all depends on where I can get satisfying work," Dad said simply.

"Are you worried, son?" Big Dad asked.

"I'd be foolish not to be," Dad answered. "I'm good at what I do, but I may not be as good as a couple of other people who want the same job."

"Well, you know we'll help out in whatever way we can."

"Thanks. It's good to know that, believe me."

From there, the conversation turned to other topics, including the trip to Florida that Gran and Big Dad planned for November. Hill was going to house-sit for two weeks while they were gone.

"So you trust him not to bring hordes of teenagers in to tear up everything?" Dad asked.

"The very idea!" Gran was indignant. "Hill would never do such a thing. He's a wonderful boy. The biggest help. Why, last year he . . ." and she launched into a catalogue of Hill's virtues as a household helper. Arden caught Dad's eye again, but he merely smiled.

"You think Joan raised him right, then," he said when Gran had finally run down.

"Well, I suppose so. Didn't you have anything to do with it?"

"Sure. But it was Joan's idea to make sure he knew how to take care of stuff around the house. You know I was never very good at that, in my younger days."

"Because your mother waited on you hand and foot," Big Dad muttered, risking a sharp look from Gran.

"Well, whoever is responsible, he's a fine young man," Gran said, standing up. "He's going places in this world. Now I'm going to get dinner on the table. Excuse me."

Arden knew that even if she went right now and set the table, Gran wouldn't make a fuss about it because that was what girls were expected to do. Gran never raved on about how wonderful *she* was. Well, then, as long as she was going to be disappointed anyhow, Arden would give her good reason. She didn't move from her chair.

As though he could read Arden's thoughts, Dad said, "I think I'll surprise Mother and help her with dinner."

"She won't let you." Big Dad laughed. "She'll chase you out of the kitchen."

"I'll bet she won't. I'll tell her I want to talk to her."

"Good luck," Big Dad said, with his wheezing chuckle. "I'll be looking for you back here in one minute."

Dad went to the kitchen and left Arden with Big Dad sitting on the back porch. In the afternoon heat, the glass in Arden's hand sweated and dripped on her shorts. She took a drink of lemonade, trying to pretend that she didn't feel guilty.

"Your dad must've cast a magic spell over your grandmother," Big Dad said.

Arden tried to smile, but her face wouldn't cooperate.

"How are you feeling about all this change?" he asked her. His quiet, rumbly voice was soothing.

"Bad," she said. "I don't want to move. I hope we don't have to."

"I understand that," he said. "Haverlee's a nice town. I wouldn't mind living there myself."

She was surprised. "But I thought you were strictly a city person."

"Not always. I grew up in a little place in the mountains, not any bigger than Haverlee. I came here right out of high school. It was the only place I could find work then—the Great Depression, you know. I sympathize with your dad. I know what it feels like to be stranded without a job. At least then I didn't have a family to support."

"I don't like it when Gran says things about Haverlee,"

Arden said suddenly. "Even if she thinks it, I wish she wouldn't say it. It makes me mad, and I'm not allowed to talk back."

"She doesn't mean anything by it," Big Dad said. "Your grandmother never was one to hold back her opinions. But it's all right for you to speak up in defense of your town, if you can do it politely. Believe me, the last thing in the world she wants to do is to hurt your feelings. She loves you a lot, Arden. You're the only girl in the family for two generations."

Arden sighed. "Well, does she love me for me, or because I'm the only girl?"

Big Dad laughed. "Both, I expect. It's been hard for her, having to put up with so many males. I guess she wants to be sure that her only female grandchild doesn't turn out to be just another boy."

Arden blinked. "How could I? I'm a girl!"

"I know. But your grandmother has definite ideas about what boys do and what girls do . . . and don't do."

"But," Arden argued, "she just got through raving about how well Hill does housework."

Big Dad snorted. "Your brain's too logical for a woman."

Arden knew he wasn't serious, so she wasn't insulted. She studied him as he sat relaxed in the porch chair. He was such a peaceful person. How strange that he had married Gran, who didn't seem peaceful at all.

"Most of the time it's men who think there's men's work and women's work."

"Oh, I think it, too," Big Dad said unabashedly. "I don't iron my shirts—wouldn't touch an iron with a ten-foot pole. And I don't do washing. Don't know a thing about that machine—don't want to learn."

"But what if Gran got sick? Would you just go around dirty and wrinkled?"

Big Dad laughed uproariously, slapping his knee. When he

was able, he said, "No. I'd hire someone to wash and iron."

"So then, I guess if something happened to you, Gran would have to do the same thing—hire someone."

That sobered him a little. "Yes, I suppose she would."

"Well, it'll take a lot of money. I hope you have a bundle!"

He laughed again. "Arden, you're a stitch. I never met a young'un like you in my entire life."

"Soup's on!" Dad yelled from somewhere in the depths of the house. Arden heard Gran say something sharp to him, and even though she didn't hear the words, she was almost willing to bet her last cent that Gran was telling him he shouldn't yell. Gosh, Dad was forty-three years old! A person ought to be able to yell anytime he wanted to when he got to be that old.

CHAPTER FOUR

THE VISIT WITH GRAN AND BIG DAD WASN'T AS DIFFICULT AS Arden had feared it might be. She got to stay in the blue bedroom, with all the elegant furniture, including the desk with many drawers and pokey-holes. Lolling in the four-poster bed with its satin comforter made her feel like a queen. She did not look in the tall mirror of the bureau very much, though. Somehow her braids and jeans destroyed the illusion of queenliness.

At breakfast Tuesday morning, when Dad left for an interview, Big Dad suggested to Arden that she go with him to the Senior Citizens Center, where he did volunteer work. He was their fix-it man. Anything that got broken during the week was put to one side until Big Dad came on Tuesday.

"Sure! That would be fun," she said. "I can help."

"I think it would be nice if you wore a dress," said Gran.

"To fix stuff?" Arden was incredulous. "But I'd—"

"Remember, you're not in Haverlee now," Gran said. "You

have to be a little more careful about your appearance when you go out."

With her eyes, Arden appealed to Big Dad, but for once he didn't seem to see anything wrong with Gran's request. With a sigh, she got up from the table and went upstairs. She had brought one cotton sundress with little shoulder straps. She put it on, and her sandals, gave her hair a perfunctory swipe with the brush so it wouldn't be quite so frizzy around her forehead, and went back downstairs.

"You look nice," Gran said, smiling her approval.

"Thanks," said Arden, not very graciously.

She and Big Dad spent the morning mending a broken toaster and repairing a couple of door latches. He showed her how to cut an electric wire and replace a worn plug with a new one. He showed her how to take apart an old lock, remembering where the pieces went, and how to oil the moving parts. It was all very logical and orderly. She wondered why she had ever thought these kinds of chores were mysterious and difficult. At a quarter to twelve, Big Dad put up his tools.

"Go wash the grease off your hands," he said. "We'll go home to lunch now."

She rode beside him, feeling contented and pleased with herself. Big Dad pulled into the driveway and parked the car. They both got out, and he went ahead of her to open the door.

As she walked into the living room, her eyes not yet accustomed to the indoor light, she was greeted by shouts of "Surprise! Surprise! Happy Birthday!"

She was surrounded by girls, some of whom she recognized and some she had never seen before. They all seemed to be grinning at her. Festoons of crepe paper hung from the ceiling. Balloons bobbed from light fixtures. A large banner reading HAPPY BIRTHDAY, ARDEN was draped across an entire wall.

"Oh, my!" she murmured, not knowing what to do. Her real birthday was three days from now. She had never dreamed of anything like this. Gran suddenly appeared at her elbow, looking enormously pleased. Big Dad was nowhere in sight. Arden felt like a bug pinned to cotton. Painfully aware of her sweaty face and the black stains under her fingernails, she thought the town girls looked fresh, cool, and older somehow.

"Arden, I thought perhaps you'd had enough of us old folks, so I invited some of the girls for a birthday lunch," Gran said, taking her arm. "Let me introduce you. Kim and Theresa and Beth you already know. And here are Barbara, Emmy Lou, and Cindy. I've known these girls since they were babies. As a matter of fact, I knew their mothers when *they* were babies."

"Hello," said Arden. She tried to smile. "I'm glad to see you."

She didn't mean it. She longed to be somewhere—any-where—else. These girls seemed to be waiting for her to do or say something clever. She saw now why Gran had wanted her to wear a dress today.

"I don't know what to say," she said. "You took me by surprise."

"That's what we meant to do," said Theresa. "We were afraid your granddad would tell."

"Well, he didn't." She felt partly betrayed by him. She started to add that if he had told her, she'd have jumped out of the car and run away, but somehow she knew that wouldn't go over very well, even as a joke.

After an awkward silence, Gran insisted that they all go to the dining room. They moved forward, crowding around the table. Each plate held chicken salad, tomatoes, little crustless sandwiches, melon balls, and rolls—a regular ladies' lunch-

32

eon. In the middle of the table was a huge bouquet of colorful late-summer flowers. Arden looked around at the bright tones and soft pastels of the girls' dresses. They were like flowers, too. She did not feel like a flower at all.

One by one, they found their places with the help of place-cards. "Here's your name, Arden," Kim said. Her smooth blond hair was pulled back and pinned loosely. "Right next to mine."

Arden went around the table to the chair beside Kim's. At least she would be next to someone she knew. Full of apprehension, she pulled out the chair and sat down.

Once again, all eyes were on her, and she realized with sudden panic that she was the hostess. She would have to be the person who did everything first . . . and right. Her eyes sought Gran's, who hovered in the background with a pitcher of lemonade, but Gran only smiled and nodded as if to say, You're on your own.

Table manners. Hands in lap. Take napkin, unfold it and put it in lap. Arden was aware as she did this that the others followed her lead. She surveyed the silverware, all properly laid out. Two little forks. That meant a salad and then dessert. She chose the outside fork as she had been taught, and everyone did the same. It wasn't so bad once they started eating. She supposed that if this were a real test, she would have to be responsible for the conversation, too, but that wasn't necessary. All the town girls knew one another. They talked about starting junior high, a place called Brinks. Arden was quite satisfied for them to rattle on. It allowed her to eat.

But the reprieve didn't last. "Tell us about you, Arden," said Barbara from across the table. She was very tan, with glossy black hair cut close to her ears. A thin gold chain gleamed at her neck. "I've heard about your cute brother!"

She rolled her eyes and giggled. Some of the others did, too. Arden wondered what Hill would say if she told him a bunch of seventh graders had crushes on him.

"What do you want to know?" she asked.

"Have you got a boyfriend?" Emmy Lou asked. Arden noted that she had a lot of green stuff around her eyes.

"No!" Arden said emphatically.

"Well, what do you like to do?" This was Cindy. Arden realized that none of the town girls she'd played with in her growing-up years asked her any questions.

"Read. Skate," she said. She couldn't think what to say beyond that.

"Do you take dancing or swimming?"

"No."

Beth frowned slightly. "Don't you do anything for fun?"

Arden looked at Beth's round face and bright blue eyes. How could she explain? "Everything is fun," she said. "I don't think about having to do special things for fun." She looked down at her plate. She had eaten all of her food, so she couldn't retreat behind a full mouth. No one else's plate was empty. In the far corner of her mind, she recalled Gran admonishing her once about eating too fast. If you were the hostess, Gran had said, you would continue to eat for as long as any one of your guests was still eating. That means you have to have something on your plate. You can't wolf it down.

"May I have another roll, please?" she said, and when the bread basket was passed, she spent a long time breaking the roll, buttering a little piece, and chewing. The conversation among the other girls resumed. Gran came and went, pouring lemonade, bringing more rolls, hovering. The girls didn't seem to mind her being there, but then, she wasn't checking on *their* table manners. Arden's head began to ache a little behind her right eye.

34

When Gran came to remove the luncheon plates, Arden offered to help, but Gran waved her back. "No, you girls just enjoy yourselves."

Arden slumped back into the chair, smothering a sigh. Probably Gran was the only one actually enjoying herself. The town girls didn't want to be there. They were only doing Gran a favor. And Arden certainly didn't want to be there. She was trapped.

"Happy birthday to you! Happy birthday to you!" Gran sang from the doorway. The other girls joined in as she bore an enormous yellow birthday cake into the dining room. The candle flames stretched backward in the breeze as she moved. She set it directly in front of Arden, along with a silver cake cutter.

"Make a wish, Arden," Theresa said. "And don't tell."

Don't worry, Arden thought. But she knew her wish. It was the only one she ever had these days—that her family wouldn't have to move from Haverlee.

Gran had spread thirteen candles plus one-to-grow-on all over the cake's surface, so that blowing them out would not be easy. Ordinarily that would not have bothered her, but this wish was crucial. She felt she must blow out all the candles at once. She took a breath so deep it almost made her dizzy, and blew.

One candle still burned. She blew it out with a puff, full of disappointment.

"That's all right," said Kim in her ear, as the others laughed and clapped. "That only means it'll take an extra year for it to come true."

"It can't wait that long," Arden muttered, but no one heard.

"Now, Arden, you may cut the cake," Gran said, setting a stack of dessert plates beside her.

"Please—I'd rather not," Arden said. "I'm no good at this."

"Nonsense!" Gran laughed. "You'll do fine."

Arden took up the silver cake cutter, clutching the handle as if it were an ax. Angry at Gran, she surveyed the cake, trying to figure out what size and shape the pieces should be. Grimly, she sliced into it, serving one piece after another. The sugary icing was thick and gooey on her fingers. When the last slice was cut, she stood up abruptly.

"Excuse me—I have to wash this mess off my hands," she announced, and headed for the kitchen. Gran was just coming out with a wet cloth.

"Oh—I was bringing something—"

"My hands are sticky." Arden brushed past her. "I have to wash them."

"But your guests are—"

"I don't plan to spend the day in here!" Arden mumbled, needing to say it, but hoping Gran didn't hear. She turned the kitchen tap on full blast and rubbed her hands together under the stream of water, wishing with all her heart that she didn't have to go back in there. The headache was now throbbing in earnest. She sighed and turned off the water, looking around for something to dry her hands on. Gran had removed all the everyday towels and cloths. Little fancy BoPeep kinds of things were hanging all around.

Gran appeared in the doorway. "Come on, Arden. Your guests are waiting."

"I'm looking for something to dry my hands on!" she said crossly. Immediately she saw the slight tightening of Gran's mouth that signaled hurt.

"Here." Gran handed her one of the fancy towels and she dried her hands. "You've got water drops all over the front of your dress."

"They'll dry," she said curtly. Imagine worrying about little old water drops!

Back in the dining room, the girls sat politely with their slices of cake in front of them, waiting for her to sit down. She felt like yelling at them, but of course she could not. She took her place, mumbled an apology, and did what was expected of her.

When dessert was finished, Gran herded them to the living room. Arden hung back. Oh, Dad—come get me, she thought. Let's go home!

But it wasn't over yet. When she entered the living room at last, there was Gran's card table in the middle of everything, and on it were gaily wrapped gifts of all sizes. Her heart sank. How could Gran have allowed it? People shouldn't have to give gifts to folks they don't know.

She went through the business of unwrapping each gift, looking pleased, and thanking each giver. There was a box of stationery with blue flowers on it, a silver neck chain, a bottle of cologne, a book with a funny cover called *Teenage Romance*, a little box with eye shadow in it, and a five-year diary. She felt that she was unwrapping someone else's presents, not her own. When she had opened the last one, she thanked them politely, wondering if they could tell what she was really thinking.

"There *is* one more gift," said Gran, reaching behind her chair and bringing forth a large box wrapped in silver and blue. "It's from me."

Arden took the box in both hands. It was about the size and shape for something to wear. She was careful with the paper. DorJo would like to have it. The white box bore the name of an expensive store. The girls hovered as she lifted the lid and parted the tissue paper. Nestled in it was something soft and blue. She lifted it out to the accompaniment of squeals and sighs from the other girls.

"Oh, wow! It's a Danielle!" Theresa moaned reverently.

She touched the blue material. "It's so gorgeous. What a marvelous gran you have!"

"What's a Danielle?" Arden asked.

"What's a Danielle? You mean you've never heard of a Danielle?"

"I mean I never have," Arden said, suddenly overcome with a great need to laugh. She looked at the dress she held in her hand. It looked elegant, like something a person would wear to a formal banquet or a concert. It would require special shoes. There was no place in Haverlee to wear an outfit like this.

"It's beautiful, Gran," she said. She got up and went over to kiss Gran's cheek.

"I can't wait to see you in it," Gran said, smiling. "As soon as I saw it, I knew it was you."

If you think this is me, then you don't know me at all, Arden thought.

Returning to her seat, she carefully put the dress back into the box, shrouded it with tissue paper, and closed the lid.

The girls stayed only a few minutes longer, then their parents came to pick them up. When the last one had gone, the house was blessedly quiet. Gran closed the front door, watched Kim go down the steps, then sighed with satisfaction.

"Such a nice group of girls, aren't they?" she said to Arden.

"Yes, ma'am."

"If you and your family *do* move to Grierson, I hope you'll cultivate their friendship," Gran went on, moving toward the dining table to begin clearing away the party debris.

Arden remained silent. She scraped cake scraps out of the dessert plates and stacked them. I am not moving to Grierson, she thought. I'd rather die.

"Do you really like the dress?" Gran asked.

"Yes, ma'am. I've never had anything quite so fancy, though."

"You probably think you have nowhere to wear a dress like that, but it works the other way around. First you get the outfit, then you look for places to wear it. The next time you come for a visit, we'll go someplace where you can wear it."

"All right," said Arden. Gran didn't seem to notice her lack of enthusiasm.

"Would you mind trying it on?" Gran said. "If it doesn't fit, I'll need to exchange it."

"But I should help you clean up—"

"Pshaw—I don't have another thing to do today. Run and try it on. Your granddad will want to see you in it."

I'll just bet he will, Arden thought sourly as she trudged upstairs with the large box. In the blue bedroom, she opened it once more. She lifted out the dress by its shoulders, looking at it more carefully than she had at first. The material was so thin a person could see right through it. The softly pleated skirt would swish and swing when she walked. She realized that with this kind of dress, a person had to have on more underwear than she happened to have. She hadn't brought a slip with her. Well, too bad. She'd just have to tell Gran.

But as usual, Gran had a solution. She directed Arden to get a slip from her own bureau drawer.

Arden went back upstairs, even more slowly this time. She found a slip among Gran's lacy lingerie and took it back to the blue room. When she put it on, she felt like a welfare child. Gran had a bosom. The slip pooched out under Arden's armpits. It hung below her knees. She worked for a minute or two on the adjustable straps, trying to make the slip shorter, but when she did, the top of it came almost to her neck. She could feel her patience slipping away like a ball of yarn coming unwound.

"Oh, shoot!" She yanked up the blue dress from the bed, not even trying to be careful with it anymore. She pulled it down over her head and arms, tugging and pulling as though she were wrestling a monster in a bag. By the time it was on and each tiny button fastened, she was sweating. Looking in the mirror she saw that her face was damp, the little ringlets of hair around it dark with perspiration. The blue dress was still pretty, and it fit, but the wrong person was wearing it. Theresa or Kim would look great in something like this, cool and neat as they were, but she just looked like a person wearing someone else's clothes.

Gran's slip was showing, too. Without bothering to make herself look better, she stomped downstairs.

"Here it is," she announced, striding into the kitchen where Gran was already washing dishes. She simply stood and let Gran get her eyes full.

"Well," said Gran after a moment, taking her hands out of the dishwater, "it's the right size, isn't it?"

"Yes, ma'am. It fits all right."

"But, of course, having to wear my slip doesn't do anything for the dress." She dried her hands and came over, turning Arden around so she could inspect the lines, the shoulder width, the skirt length. Arden bore it as long as she could.

"May I take it off now?" she said finally. "It's hot!"

"I'd like for Jake to see it. Wait a minute." Gran went to the top of the basement stairs and called down. "Jake—come up here and see Arden's new dress!"

There was a pause, during which Big Dad hollered something that Arden couldn't quite hear, but Gran did.

"No, she can't come down there! She'd get grease or dirt on it and we'd never get it out."

Another pause, then Gran said, "He's coming."

Arden endured the wait while Big Dad took his time coming up the steep basement stairs. He caught sight of her when he was about three steps from the top.

"My Lord, Arden, your slip's showing a mile!" he said.

She burst out laughing. Gran looked disgusted.

"Jake, I declare you don't have any sensitivity at all," she scolded. "It's my slip, if you want to know. You aren't supposed to be looking at the slip anyway—look at the dress!"

"It's hard *not* to look at the slip," Big Dad said. "It's practically dragging the floor."

Arden put her hand over her mouth to smother the giggles. Big Dad tilted his head to one side and looked at the dress as he had been instructed to do.

"Well," he said after a moment, "it's a pretty dress, no doubt. It just doesn't look like something Arden would've picked out for herself."

"Of course not!" Gran fussed. She went back to the sink to attack the dishes. "That's the whole point."

"Oh," said Big Dad. "Well, it's a pretty dress, like I said."

"May I go take it off now, Gran?" Arden asked again. "It's getting all sweaty."

"Sure. Go right ahead." Arden saw that Gran's mouth trembled ever so slightly, as though she might be about to cry. Gran never cried. Suddenly, Arden felt awful. Gran had done a great deal for her today, and so far she had mostly griped about it. She went over and kissed Gran's cheek.

"You wait," she said. "When I get cleaned up and have on my own slip, it'll look lots better."

Gran nodded, somewhat mollified. Big Dad came up the steps into the kitchen.

"I've got something for you, too," he said. "When you've changed your clothes, I'll give it to you."

A half hour later, she was back in the kitchen, comfortable in her shorts. All of her belongings were packed and ready in a little bundle on the great bed in the blue room. She hoped Dad would want to leave the minute he returned.

"I put your gifts in a box by the door," Gran said. "I included a list of the girls' names and addresses. You should write to each of them before the end of the week, to thank them."

"Yes, ma'am." She suppressed a sigh. She hadn't asked for the party or the presents. Why did she have to be punished? That's what writing thank-you notes felt like—punishment.

Big Dad came in again, this time with a box in his hand that wasn't even wrapped. "This won't be much of a surprise. The day we went fishing, you said it was what you wanted."

Arden took the box from him. Inside was a very fine pocketknife, with a strong handle and several blades. She took it out and hefted it in her palm. She liked its weight, its no-nonsense appearance. One by one, she opened the blades until they were all out—a pen blade, a file, a combination bottle opener and flathead screwdriver, a fish scaler, and a smaller pen blade.

"Big Dad, it's perfect. It's even better than I imagined. Thanks!" She gave him a great hug.

"Well," said Gran in a funny voice, "I guess I've learned my lesson."

Arden whirled to look at her. "What?"

"That it's a waste of time to try to surprise people with something you think they ought to like. When they tell you what they want, you should listen to them."

"But Gran, just because I like the knife doesn't mean I don't like what you did for me."

"You can't fool me, Arden. Especially not you—you're too honest. I can see the difference between real enthusiasm and politeness."

"Sally, don't make Arden feel bad," Big Dad said. "That's not fair."

"I don't mean to make her feel bad. I just learned an important lesson."

42

"Look," said Arden, trying to put a better face on things. "What you did today was good for me. You know how hard it is for me to be proper. If it was up to me, I'd never in a million years get into a situation where I had to know my manners. But I guess I do need to know."

To her surprise, Gran actually smiled warmly at her. "Well, I have to say that I was very proud of you today, Arden. You were a perfect hostess. I apologize for putting you on the spot."

Without a word, Big Dad went over to Gran and put both arms around her. He hugged and kissed her as though Arden were not standing right there watching.

"Sally, you are a wonderful woman!" he pronounced. "I defy anyone to say otherwise."

"Oh, Jake—quit being foolish!" But Gran hugged him back and her eyes got watery.

Arden and Gran finished cleaning up the kitchen with a much better spirit between them. When Dad came back about three o'clock, she was content to wait while he reported to Gran and Big Dad what he had done and the people he had seen.

"You're hopeful, then?" Big Dad asked.

"More than I was. At least I'm doing something."

"I'll keep my eyes and ears open," Big Dad said. "Sometimes it isn't *what* you know, but *who* you know."

"Whom," said Gran automatically. Everyone laughed.

On the way home, Arden told Dad about everything that had happened, including Gran's hurt feelings. She told how Gran had apologized to her. "I never thought I'd see the day that Gran would admit to making a mistake," she said, still wondering at it.

"Did she make a mistake?" Dad asked.

"Well, it was like she said—she put me on the spot. I could've really goofed."

"But you didn't?"

Arden wrinkled her nose and grinned. "I must not have. She said I was a perfect hostess."

Dad laughed and reached over to pat her knee. "I'm proud of you, Bird. It must have been hard, but I appreciate your doing your best for Gran's sake. She's an unusual person. You'll find it out one of these days."

Arden looked out the window. She never liked it when grownups implied that you weren't old enough or smart enough to see what was right in front of your face.

CHAPTER FIVE

ARDEN'S THIRTEENTH BIRTHDAY CAME AND WENT, LEAVING her unchanged so far as she could tell. Of course, DorJo had already been thirteen almost a whole year and had never acted strange, at least not until the trip to camp. Since her own birthday, Arden had felt a bit cautious when she woke up each morning, thinking it might be the very day when the change would begin in earnest. So far, though, she was reassured by what she saw in the mirror: same braids, same jeans and comfortable shirts, same unadorned face. The presents she had received from the town girls lay packed in a bottom drawer, unused.

Some things around her had changed, though. When school started, she had two teachers instead of one. Miss Brill taught science and math in the mornings, and Mrs. Haley taught language arts and social studies in the afternoon. Arden, always a good student, found herself struggling for A's from Miss Brill. More than once, she wished that Hill was still around to help with homework.

For the first time in her life, Arden didn't have any classes with DorJo and Seth. Although they didn't talk about it among themselves, all three knew that Arden had been placed in the class with the best students. Arden missed her friends more than she had imagined was possible, especially DorJo. They walked to and from school together every day and met at lunchtime in the cafeteria, but the enforced separation had its effect. If something happened in class that was funny, frightening, or embarrassing, it took Arden a lot more time to tell about it. Most of the time, she found she could not do justice to the incident in the telling. DorJo would listen politely and then say, "I guess you had to be there, huh?"

The three of them escaped to the pond behind Seth's house as often as they could manage, but somehow they didn't have as much free time as they used to. It took longer to do homework, and all their parents seemed to expect more of them this year.

But one rare day in late September, they were all free at the same time. Giddy with their good fortune, laughing and acting silly, they clambered aboard Seth's homemade raft and poled out to the middle of the pond. DorJo heaved overboard the rusted chunk of iron that had once been part of a car engine but was now their anchor. The thick rope to which it was tied uncoiled and slithered after the anchor like a fat, hairy snake. Then she flopped down on the splintery planks, hunching her shoulders forward so that more of the September sun could warm her back.

Seth lifted the long pole out of the water and laid it carefully along one end of the raft. He lay down on his back and squinted up at the clear sky. Arden noted that his hair, which had once been almost cotton white, had begun to darken some. She realized, too, that he had grown since last year. He was as tall as she was now, although that still wasn't saying much.

46

She stretched out on her stomach, propping herself up on her elbows so that she could look at the grassy shore across the expanse of greenish water. A slight breeze rippled the pond and the raft bobbed lightly. The soft lapping at the raft's edge was, she thought, just about the most comforting sound in all creation.

"Has your dad got a job yet?" Seth asked.

Instantly the feeling of security shattered to bits. "No," she said shortly.

Silence followed. It stretched and grew until it covered the raft and spilled over into the pond. Arden imagined it like a sticky veil settling over them all forever.

"I hate to see you have to move," Seth said finally with a wistful sigh. "I wish—"

"I'm not gone yet!" she interrupted, raising her voice. "There's still a chance I won't have to go. People shouldn't give up so easily!"

Seth rolled over on his side and looked at her. "Okay, okay! I didn't mean I'd give up on you."

"It sounded that way." She turned her back on him. "DorJo already said I could live with them anyhow."

Seth brightened. "Sure enough?" He turned to DorJo. "Hey, that's great!"

DorJo didn't say anything. With her index finger, she traced the outline on a knothole in one of the pine planks. An uneasy suspicion arose in Arden's mind.

"Have you come right out and asked your mama, Dor?"

"I don't need to," DorJo said brusquely. "I know she won't mind."

Arden felt that something that had been solid under her had suddenly been withdrawn. "I wouldn't expect her to do it for nothing," she said. "Dad would pay for my food and all, and my share of . . . of everything."

47

"I know that!" DorJo threw a wood chip into the water with an angry gesture. "I told you she wouldn't mind. Don't you believe me?"

"Well, I just wouldn't want to surprise her with the idea at the last minute," Arden said. "If she has a longer time to think about it, she might be more in favor. My folks always think of reasons *not* to do something first. Good arguing takes time."

"Mama isn't like your folks," DorJo said. "Let me do it my way."

"I've been making wishes on everything I could find," Seth said. "On the first star, on matches, on—"

"Aw, Seth—that's just superstition," Arden scoffed.

Unoffended, Seth shrugged. "You don't know. You can't ever tell when a wish'll take hold somewhere and change things around. It sure ain't going to *hurt*."

There was no arguing the point. Arden was glad that Seth cared enough about her staying to make it the focus of his wishing. After all, he had more important things he could be wishing for, like a healthy heart or a few extra inches in height.

Later, as she and DorJo walked home from Seth's, they talked about what might happen.

"The truth is, the chances that we'll stay here get slimmer every day," Arden said. "I keep hoping, but there's not much to go on."

"I was thinking," DorJo said hesitantly, "that maybe you could pray to God not to make your family move."

Arden turned her head swiftly to look at her friend. She had never heard DorJo comment on such things before.

"Well, when I was at camp, people prayed a lot," DorJo stumbled on, obviously uncomfortable.

The suggestion was unsettling to Arden. Sure, she said grace at table, and she had learned prayers when she was little, most of which she still said by heart. Her family had always been members of the Methodist Church. But praying about this moving business seemed to her to be a bit forward. You just couldn't ask for something big like that without building up to it.

"I don't know," she said. "How would I . . . I mean, I don't know if a person should pray for something like that."

"Well, what else is there to pray for?" DorJo said, turning her palms up. "What's the use of praying for what you can get all by yourself?"

The way DorJo talked, there didn't seem to be much difference between wishing on a star and praying. Except that praying was more respectable. Even grownups confessed to doing it, whereas almost no one over twelve would admit to serious wishing.

"Are you praying for Mark to like you?" she asked DorJo, because she really wanted to know whether it worked.

DorJo turned beet red. "I guess so, a little." She bent suddenly in mid-stride and picked up a stick from the ground. She wouldn't look at Arden but walked on, tapping the stick on the ground at every third step.

"Well, how can you tell if it works? I mean, will you get a letter from Mark, or what?"

"I don't know!" DorJo flared unexpectedly. "Why don't you just forget I mentioned it, huh?"

It dawned on Arden that DorJo was embarrassed. "Yeah—okay," she said quietly.

Still, after they parted and Arden continued home alone, she couldn't dismiss DorJo's suggestion completely. Maybe it was high time she started paying attention to things like that. Maybe if she had been a better person, Dad wouldn't be losing his job and they would be living in Haverlee forever.

On impulse, she turned in at the Methodist Church and went along the brick walkway to the front entrance. The large wooden double doors were not locked. She pressed the brass thumb latch and the door opened inward. A rush of cool, stale air greeted her. Stepping inside quickly, she closed the door behind her.

The sanctuary was dim. It was the first time she had ever been here when there wasn't something going on. Without a lot of people around, the place was strange and watchful, as though spirits might be in charge. It gave her a funny feeling—not really scared, but odd and out of place.

She sat down in one of the pews and looked around. If a person *did* want a quiet place, this sure filled the bill. It was so quiet she could hear her own breathing. But how did a person go about praying? She felt self-conscious saying anything aloud, so she thought it as hard as she could.

You must know, she thought, how much I want to stay in Haverlee. If there's any way in the world You can improve business at EZ Life Appliances, the problem would be solved. I'd certainly appreciate it. I will also try to do better about my praying and all.

And then, after a moment's hesitation, she thought, Amen.

Well, I guess I will go now.

She didn't know whom she was explaining that to, since no one was around. She got up and walked out the way she had come, feeling that something wasn't finished.

Mom and Dad were already eating dinner when she got home.

"Better hurry up!" Dad called to her from the kitchen. "Your mom and I are about to divide your share between us."

"You better not!" she hollered back, as she ducked into the downstairs bathroom to wash her hands. At least Dad was in a good mood. These days it was hard to predict how he would be at dinnertime. When he was depressed, everyone's spirits slid downhill.

"Where've you been all this time?" Mom asked, as Arden slipped into her place at the table.

"We were out on Seth's pond. First time in days. None of us wanted to leave."

Dad smiled. He really did seem to be in a good mood tonight. He and Mom passed the serving bowls to Arden and she piled her plate high. The roast chicken and rice made her mouth water.

For a few minutes, she concentrated on eating, half listening to Mom's and Dad's conversation. They talked about Gran's and Big Dad's trip to Florida. It seemed to her that they were inordinately interested in the exact times of her grandparents' departure and return.

"You're not worried about Hill being there alone, are you?" she asked. "Gran already said *they're* not worried."

"No," said Dad. "We were just—" He stopped and looked over at Mom. "Well, the truth is, I have some news."

Arden stopped chewing. Everything stopped.

"What?"

"I got word this morning that EZ Life wants me at the Grierson plant," Dad said, smiling.

At the same moment, Arden thought she distinctly heard a door slam. "Oh," she said in a small, faraway voice. There was a kind of roaring noise that made hearing difficult. "You must be glad." She kept looking at the smile on his face. She hated the smile because it was real.

"Yes, I truly am." He reached over and covered her hand with his. "I didn't realize until I heard they wanted me how scared I was that they wouldn't."

She struggled for something appropriate to say, but her head wasn't working right. Mom was looking at her with the same concerned expression she used when one of them had a fever.

"I guess that means . . . we move to Grierson." The words were blocks of wood coming out of her mouth, hard and painful.

Dad nodded. Now the smile was gone. He squeezed her hand. "Yes. Gran and Big Dad will help us find a house in a good neighborhood. I called them today to let them know."

"You . . . you aren't going to try to move there before December, are you?"

"No," said Mom firmly. "We definitely won't leave until after Christmas. I promised the hospital I'd stay until then, and your dad and Mr. Briggs have to oversee the plant closing here."

"Is Mr. Briggs moving to Grierson, too?" She didn't really care. She didn't even know why she asked the question, but Dad's response surprised her.

"No, he isn't."

"Where's he going, then?"

"I don't know." Dad looked grim. "EZ Life had one opening in Grierson. I got it."

"That's awful!"

"Yes," he admitted. "I know how I'd feel if things were the other way around."

Arden looked at the food left on her plate. None of Seth's wishes had, after all, taken hold. Her attempt at praying had apparently been to no purpose. Maybe she had made God mad today, bopping into church with no preparation as she had done. She wondered whether Dad and Mr. Briggs had prayed. If so, had God chosen one to win and one to lose?

"A penny for your thoughts," Mom said gently.

52

Arden glanced up. She felt herself coming back from a great distance.

"Nothing," she said, aware that her reply didn't fit. But it was what she felt. They could move if they wanted to. She did not intend to go. She had three months to figure out how she would stay.

CHAPTER SIX

IT WAS THE FIRST DAY OF NOVEMBER. LATE IN THE AFTERNOON, the telephone rang and Arden got up from doing her homework to answer it.

"Arden?" said the voice at the other end.

"Yes." She didn't quite recognize the voice.

"I need to speak to Dad."

"Hill! I didn't know who you were. You sound funny—"

"Is Dad there?"

"Yes, of course." She was a little miffed at him for not even asking how she was. "I think he's outside. You want to wait a minute while I get him, or do you want him to call you back? Or will you speak with Mom?"

"Arden, get Dad . . . it's important." Something in Hill's tone made her feel odd.

"Hold on," she said, subdued. She put the receiver on the table and ran through the house calling Dad.

"He's in the backyard," Mom said, as Arden passed through the kitchen. "What is it?"

"Hill's on the phone. Says he has to talk to Dad." She opened the back door and went out. The chill wind made her eyes water. Dad was by the back fence, piling discarded boxes beside the trashcan.

"Dad, Hill's on the phone!" she called. "He says it's important!"

"Coming." He started toward the house, not particularly hurrying. For some reason she wanted to jump up and down and shout at him to run, but she had no reason to do such a thing. She waited shivering until he reached the porch.

"You shouldn't be out here without a sweater," Dad said, as he passed her. "What does Hill want?"

"He didn't say." She followed at his heels through the house and hovered nearby as Dad picked up the receiver and spoke into it.

"Hill? What's up?"

She watched him listen. Before her very eyes, his face lengthened and turned gray. "No!" The word burst from his mouth.

Frightened, Arden turned and ran to the kitchen. "Mom— come quick. I think it's real bad news!"

Mom grabbed a towel to wipe her hands and came after her. When they got back to the hall, Dad was speaking into the mouthpiece. His voice was thin and shaky.

"Hill, I'll leave as soon as I can. I'll be there before midnight. Stay with Mother. Good boy. I love you."

Arden heard the click as Hill hung up, but Dad held on to the receiver and stared ahead of him. He shook his head slightly, as though to deny what he had heard. Arden held Mom's arm without even realizing it.

"What is it, Tom?" Mom asked quietly.

"Dad's dead."

"Oh, no!" Mom's voice was anguished. She moved swiftly

to put her arms around Dad, hugging him hard. Very carefully, he set the receiver in its place and bent his head. His face crumpled and lost its shape. Tears filled his eyes and ran down his cheeks.

Frozen to the spot, Arden felt that a great dark funnel had descended and sucked all life out of her. Big Dad dead? It could not be. But Dad was crying and so was Mom. Arden did not cry. She shivered.

"Arden." Dad held out his arms to her. She moved then, and in another moment was enveloped in his arms and Mom's. The three of them stood there, locked together, but Arden's eyes were dry. A terrible fear filled every corner of her being. She felt herself stiffening, as though the fear had begun to set.

"What happened?" she whispered.

"Hill says he had a heart attack. He was raking leaves. Mother found him out there . . . in the leaves." Dad's voice broke. His body shook. Arden was terrified by his sorrow.

"Then Mother Gifford . . . then he was already . . . gone . . . by the time she found him?" Mom asked.

"Yes. Hill says she's blaming herself. She had insisted that the leaves be raked today, so that would be done before they left for Florida. I told him to stay with her until I get there. I have to leave, Joan."

"Of course, hon." She kissed his cheek. "I'll finish fixing dinner while you get some clothes together. You go ahead tonight and Arden and I will come in the morning."

"I should call Briggs."

"Don't worry about that. I'll take care of it."

So they began to move about in a kind of quiet, gray dance. Dad called Uncle Bob in California. Arden, inside her cage of fear, did what she was told. She set the table. She brought the clean clothes upstairs so Dad could pack his suitcase. When she had done everything, she felt lost.

Dad came downstairs to the kitchen. He seemed lost, too. "How will you and Arden get there tomorrow if I take the car?" he said.

"Someone here will have one I can borrow," Mom said. "I've already thought about the people I'm going to call. Don't worry about it."

Arden's thoughts turned unbidden to Big Dad lying in the leaves. She imagined him lying with his face turned toward the November sky, the leaves making a soft bed beneath him. But perhaps he had fallen face down. What had he thought? Had he called out? And Gran was in the kitchen cooking dinner, not having any idea at all that something was wrong. The fear in Arden sloshed high like a wave and subsided. She thought about Hill. Was he scared, too? Even if he was, he would have to act like a grownup. Did he know what to do?

"Arden, are you all right?" Mom asked once.

"Yes," she said, because she couldn't think what else to say. She was still walking around, still breathing, still able to do things—so she must be all right. Then she added, "I never saw Dad cry."

"Well, your Dad loves . . . loved Big Dad very much," Mom said gently. "They have always been great friends."

Mom's words startled Arden. She had not thought about fathers and sons being friends.

"It's hard for your dad because Big Dad died so suddenly," Mom went on. "I'm glad he lets himself go ahead and cry. Some men wouldn't, you know. Did it frighten you?"

"I guess, a little." She was ashamed to admit it.

Mom gave her a hug. "Don't worry about your dad—he's as strong as he ever was, but even strong people have to grieve. If you love someone and lose them, it hurts."

Then why don't I hurt? Arden thought. Mom and Dad had both cried, but she had not done so. When she thought about

Big Dad, she couldn't cry. Did that mean she hadn't loved him?

It was dark when Dad left for Grierson. Arden and Mom hugged him one last time and then stood on the front porch until he had driven away.

"I need to tell DorJo," Arden said. "Would it be all right if I went over there now?"

Mom frowned. "I don't like the idea of you walking alone in the dark. I wish DorJo and her mother had a telephone."

"Well, they don't. And if I don't let DorJo know, she'll be expecting me to show up to walk to school tomorrow."

"All right then. Come inside and get the flashlight."

Arden knew that she could find her way in the dark, perhaps even with her eyes closed, but if it made Mom feel better for her to take a flashlight, then she would do it.

The night was still and cold. The trees were not completely bare, but one more windy day, and the oaks and maples would be skeletons. Haverlee had few streetlights—only one at each corner—but their purplish glow gave the leaves that had already fallen a strange color. Again she thought of Big Dad lying in the leaves. What if she found someone lying in these leaves, someone who had cried out and not been heard? Her heart thudded against her ribs. The piles and lumps of leaves took on an appearance they had not had before. She focused her eyes upward, away from the ground, telling herself to quit acting like a baby.

DorJo's house on Purdue Street was a welcome sight. Arden hastened toward it, anxious to be within the little pools of light from the Huggins's windows.

Mrs. Huggins answered her knock. "Oh—hey, Arden. What're you doin' over here this time of evening?" The girls didn't visit each other on weeknights.

"I . . . well, I had to tell DorJo. We've . . . there's some bad news."

"Oh?" Mrs. Huggins opened the screen door and stood aside to let Arden in. "What's the matter?"

Arden really wanted to tell DorJo first, but it would be impolite to say so. "My granddad died." It was the first time she'd said it. She thought the words would break her teeth, they came so hard.

"Oh," said Mrs. Huggins in a much softer voice. "I'm real sorry to hear that. You can go in DorJo's room—she's doing her homework."

Arden went to the door of DorJo's little room and tapped lightly. In another moment it opened. DorJo's mouth formed a little O of surprise. "Hey! What's up? Come on in."

Arden went in and sat on the bed. DorJo looked hard at her. "Something's wrong, ain't it?" she said to Arden.

Arden nodded. She began to feel an uncomfortable knot in her throat. "I had to come and tell you. Big Dad died this afternoon."

DorJo was shocked. "Your granpa? Oh, that's terrible! He's such a nice man."

Arden didn't know what to say. She almost corrected DorJo's grammar—he *was* a nice man—but a person would have to believe he was really gone for good to say *was*. In an instant, all the present was taken away from a person.

DorJo sat down on the bed beside her and put an arm around her. "Gosh, Arden, that's so awful. I know you love him a lot."

Again Arden had an impulse to correct DorJo's tenses. What a picky thing to think of right now! She was angry at herself. Instead she said, "I won't be at school tomorrow. I don't know how long we'll be in Grierson. Maybe you could tell Miss

Brill and Mrs. Haley, and find out what my homework assignments are."

"Sure. No problem." DorJo's look of distress would not go away. "It's too bad we're not in the same classes anymore. That way I could practically do your homework for you. What did you have to be so smart for?"

Arden smiled weakly and leaned against DorJo's comforting arm. "Baloney!" she muttered.

They sat for a few moments in silence, then DorJo said, "You must be real sad. I don't know what I'd do if Granpa died. I mean, I know he *will*—he's old, and he's been sick for a long time. But I just can't think about it." She shook her head, as though to dislodge the thoughts of death before they could get a firm hold.

Arden thought of Granpa Huggins, thin and stooped, a man who really did seem to be on his last legs and yet was still alive, while Big Dad, hale and hearty only a day ago, was dead. Where was justice? At least, if Granpa Huggins had died, no one would have been particularly shocked about it. Thinking such thoughts right in DorJo's own room made her feel guilty.

"I'd better get back home," she said, standing up. "Mom will worry if I don't go back soon."

"I wish it didn't happen," DorJo said earnestly.

"Yeah, me, too." Arden realized she hadn't told DorJo the how of it, about Big Dad lying in the leaves, but that was all right. That was the good thing about DorJo—she took what a person told her. She was never nosy.

"Come over as soon as you get back," DorJo said. They walked together to the door. Mrs. Huggins was watching TV, but she stood up and told Arden again that she was sorry.

"Tell your mother to let me know what I can do to help," she said.

Out in the darkness again, Arden hugged her jacket close to her. She didn't bother to turn on the flashlight. She wished the night would never end, that she did not have to face the next day, the trip to Grierson, the people she'd never met, the sorrow of her parents and Hill and . . . most of all . . . Gran. She remembered what Dad had said—Gran had insisted that the leaves be raked today. She knew how Gran was. When she wanted a thing done, she wanted it done. But Big Dad was no submissive little man. He would rake the leaves only if he wanted to. She hoped Gran would not take too much of the blame for what happened. If he was going to have a heart attack, he could just as easily have had it at the Senior Citizens Center or at home sitting in his easy chair.

When she got back to the house, the porch light was on and Mom's figure was silhouetted in the glass pane of the front door. She opened it as Arden stepped up on the porch.

"I'm glad you're back," she said. "Come in and see what you can do about packing clothes for the trip. You'll need a nice dress for the funeral. There will be lots of visitors at the house, so probably a couple more dresses, or skirts and blouses. Don't forget your good shoes."

"Can't I take some jeans? I'll go crazy if I have to wear dresses all the time!"

"Arden, we have to think about Gran—all right?" Mom's tone was right on the edge of stern.

"Oh, all right! But I don't see why in the world Gran would worry about me wearing jeans when Big Dad is dead!"

She shouted the last word. It echoed in her head for several seconds afterward, making her feel like an ill-mannered child.

"I don't think Gran will even notice," Mom said. "But we will do this for her, because if she *could* notice, it would be important to her. Do you understand?"

"Yes, ma'am," Arden said. Then, hoping to turn attention

away from herself, she added, "Mrs. Huggins said she'd be glad to do anything for us."

"That was nice," Mom said.

Arden went to her room and laid out all the clothes she would need for three or four days. She did not really know how long people hung around when someone died. Once everything was in her suitcase, she checked to be sure she hadn't left out any necessary items. Her eyes fell on the pocketknife that Big Dad had given her for her birthday. It lay on the chest of drawers where she had left it last night. The pocketknife went with her everywhere except to school. It was against the law to take a knife to school, but every afternoon as soon as she got home she tucked it in the pocket of her jeans. For some reason, today she hadn't.

Slowly she walked to the chest of drawers. Today, of all days, she hadn't put Big Dad's knife in her pocket. That felt to her like a betrayal. Reaching for the knife, she closed her hand over its thickness, its satisfying strength. It seemed to warm up immediately in her grasp. When she lifted it, she thought of the river, the pier, and of Big Dad sitting with his fishing pole propped between his knees, the yellow collar of his shirt waving in the erratic breeze.

With the knife in her hand, she moved carefully to the window seat. She sat there for a long time, holding the knife in one hand, cradling that hand with the other, resting them both against her chest, close to her heart, trying to comprehend that she had seen Big Dad with her real eyes for the last time.

With its draperies drawn, the house in Grierson is darker than she ever remembers. The November gray makes it even bleaker. People sit around in the living room talking softly, occasionally laughing. Gran moves about, never in one place for very long.

Uncle Bob and his family fly in from California. Arden and

Dad meet them at the airport. The two brothers look each other in the eye, then hug hard. She sees their terrible sadness.

She is surprised at the laughing. They sit at the table and tell stories of when they were little. Gran laughs, too, but then, in a spasm of sadness, she gets up and leaves the room.

It is too cold to be in the summer house, but she goes out there to swing, to be alone. She is not hidden from view because the wisteria has died back on the trellis. She sits exposed to the gray sky, a pale sun.

She thinks there should be more weeping, but she herself does not cry.

The funeral is her first. No one thinks to tell her what to expect, so she stays close to Mom and Dad, fearful that she will do something wrong. A great silver-gray limousine waits for them at the curb. When she looks at its darkly tinted windows, she thinks of a masked face. Once they are all inside it, no one will be able to see them. A man opens the door for them. They settle into the thick gray upholstery. She finds herself close to the window. She is surprised that she can see out.

At the church, they wait in the limousine. She watches other people going up the stone steps. Her mouth is dry, her heart pounds. From time to time, she glances at the others to see what their faces will tell her. She learns nothing.

The man opens the door for them again. All the other people are inside the church now. The man arranges them for the procession. Uncle Bob and Dad will walk on either side of Gran. Hill and Arden will walk beside Mom. The cousins and other relatives will follow.

From the vestibule where they wait for their cue to enter, she hears muted organ music. It makes her think of rose-colored velvet. She feels that she has cotton in her ears. The organ changes its tone. It plays "A Mighty Fortress." There is

63

a startling rumble as people rise to their feet. Gran and her two sons walk down the aisle. The others follow. At the bottom of the aisle, in the very center of things, is the great box with flowers on top. Her eyes are drawn to it. She thinks of Big Dad lying in the leaves. The thought of his lying now inside a box offends her.

They must sit in the front row with the whole congregation behind them.

The minister reads from the Bible. He reads the Twenty-third Psalm and Psalm I. She thinks about Big Dad being like a tree planted by the rivers of waters. He reads from the Gospel of John about not letting your heart be troubled. He reads from Romans about never being separated from the love of God. He reads from the Book of Revelation about the New Heaven and the New Earth. The words are dry and smooth, like wood that has been polished by much handling.

Arden would like to see Gran, but she would have to lean forward to look down the row to do so.

The minister lays aside his Bible and looks out at the congregation. He begins to talk about Big Dad. She thinks he must have known Big Dad very well. Mom chuckles at one of the stories. The congregation behind them does, too. It is a pleasant, warm sound, a shifting and softening of bodies. She looks at Hill. His eyes are full of tears. Quite suddenly her own eyes fill. The heaviness in her chest moves up to her throat. She opens her eyes wide so that the tears will not run down her cheeks. She takes a deep breath to chase the lump away. She does not want to cry in front of all these strangers. Her nose begins to run. She sniffs. In another moment, Mom is handing her a handkerchief. It makes her angry. She hates it that they expect her to cry!

The service ends with a congregational hymn. She looks at the words and hums the tune in her head, but her singing voice has dried up. She cannot make the notes. Nobody else in the family is singing either, though they look at the words in the hymnal.

The minister pronounces the benediction. She thinks they will leave now, but suddenly from nowhere, six men gather at the front around the box. It is on rollers. They turn it around and push it up the aisle toward the rear of the church. The family has to follow it past the faces in the rows.

They must travel several miles to a cemetery. It is an enormous place with softly rolling hills dotted with stones and occasional bright bunches of flowers. They sit in folding metal chairs under a tent before a hole shaped like the box. The box and its flowers are suspended above the hole in a metal frame. Imitation grass covers the red clay. Its harsh green makes the real grass look even deader than it is.

The minister says more words, reads more Scripture, says a prayer. Then he goes down the row of chairs and shakes hands with each person. His hand is thick and rough. Other people come under the tent. She watches. Some hug Gran, others shake hands. There are many red-rimmed eyes, pink noses. Her head is heavy. She would like to go home. She does not want to look at any more people, or have to be polite.

CHAPTER SEVEN

ARDEN KNEW THERE WAS TROUBLE WHEN, JUST TWO WEEKS after Big Dad's funeral, she happened upon Mom and Dad having an argument. She stood at the top of the stairs and listened to their voices coming from the open door of their bedroom.

"It's going to be tough," Dad was saying, "trying to meet house payments or pay rent there before we've sold this house. I don't think we can afford it, especially if you don't get a job right away."

"But Tom, that's *our* problem, not Mother Gifford's."

"She's lonely, Joan. It would do her good to have us around."

"But not *living* with her. That's her place. Think, Tom."

"We wouldn't be there forever—only until we get on our feet financially."

"I won't let you mention it to her!" Arden had never heard Mom so adamant. "When a person has suddenly lost a loved

66

one, they can't think clearly for a while afterward. We'd be taking advantage of her. I will not agree to it!"

Arden had no idea how much longer the argument would have lasted if she hadn't made a lot of noise coming down the hall. They hushed as she passed their door on the way to her room. She pretended that she hadn't heard a word, but in fact she was shaken by the realization that for once her parents were on absolutely opposite sides of a question.

Later that evening, when Mom had gone out to a meeting, Dad sat at his desk. He frowned and scribbled, chewed his pencil, rumpled his hair, squirmed, and mumbled to himself.

"Drat!" He threw down his pencil and stood up suddenly, pushing his chair backward with a loud, scraping noise. "It can't be done."

"What?" she asked.

"Oh, never mind." He sat down again slowly.

"I want to know," she persisted. "I live here, too."

With a sigh, he turned in the chair to face her. "I'm trying to figure out how we can rent a place of our own in Grierson before we sell or rent this house," he said. "So far, Nottingham Realty hasn't had a nibble."

"Why don't we just keep on living here, then?" Arden said. "Mom still has a job. We wouldn't starve."

"Not right away, maybe. But we'd get behind very quickly if her income was all we had. Besides, I want to work in the Grierson plant."

"Then why don't you go to Grierson to live with Gran and let Mom and me stay here until we sell the house?"

"We aren't splitting up the family. I draw the line there," Dad said firmly.

"It's already split," she argued. "Hill's been living in Grierson more than a year. Besides, it wouldn't be forever—just until the house was sold." She heard herself echoing the words he had spoken earlier in the afternoon.

Dad looked at her hard. "Have you mentioned this to your mother?"

"No. I just thought of it." And it was true—the idea had only occurred to her as she sat in the chair watching him. The more she thought about it, though, the more sensible it seemed. A certain lightness started somewhere deep within her. Perhaps this would be a way for her to stay in Haverlee a while longer.

"Well, don't," Dad said. He picked up the pencil again. "I think we should *all* go live with Gran until we sell the house. That way we'd all be together, Hill included."

"Gran might not be ready for a house full of people all of a sudden."

"She's lonely, Arden—she needs people around who love her."

"Isn't Hill enough?"

"That's asking too much of Hill. He's only eighteen."

"But what about the different ways Mom and Gran do things? You know—Gran waits on people and thinks women ought to do all the housework. And she likes for everything to be cleaned up as soon as it's messed up. It wouldn't be Mom's house at all. She couldn't do things her way anymore."

This time Dad didn't come back with a quick answer. Instead he tapped the pencil on the pile of papers, pursing his lips and frowning as though he might be seriously considering what she said.

"Well, all right," he said at last. "Maybe that's what Joan has been getting at all along, without coming right out and saying so. I suppose we'll go back to Grierson this weekend and look some more."

68

He went back to his figuring and Arden returned to her social studies, but her mind wandered. What if she and Mom *could* stay on here until the house was sold? Dad could visit on weekends. It made a lot of sense. Maybe that was the reason Dad didn't want her to mention it to Mom—she would think it made sense, too.

"Well—what sort of luck did you have?" Gran asked as soon as Mom and Dad walked in from their house-hunting expedition the following Saturday afternoon. Arden and Hill had been helping her clean Big Dad's basement workshop. It had been a strange morning for Arden, who felt caught between crying and laughing the whole time they worked and talked about Big Dad. Now Mom and Dad were back and Arden didn't know what she hoped they would say.

Dad opened the hall coat closet and took down two hangers. "Tell you in a minute," he said, helping Mom with her coat. "How about some hot tea for a couple of cold, footsore people?"

They sat around Gran's dining table with cups of hot spiced tea and some of her chocolate chip cookies.

"We went to twelve places," Mom said. She looked tired. "I counted them."

"Yes, and they were scattered all over the city," Dad added. "I'll have to confess that there at the last they sort of ran together."

"Didn't you like any of them?" Hill asked.

"Oh, sure," said Dad. "But as usual, the ones we could afford weren't in wonderful locations."

Arden sat very still.

Gran's arms rested on the table on either side of her teacup. Arden focused her attention on those arms, thinner and somehow frailer than before Big Dad died. Then her eyes moved to Gran's face, to the locked-in sorrow that lived there all the time now. Gran seemed to be thinking about something. Maybe she hadn't even heard what Mom and Dad said.

"I guess this means you have to come back next weekend," said Hill.

"Looks like it." Dad lifted his cup and drank the hot brew all at once. "Time's about to run out on us. We'll have better luck next weekend, I'm sure." He turned to Gran. "We want to take you back with us tomorrow, Mother, so you can be with us for Thanksgiving. I'll bring you home on Saturday, when we come back to look some more."

Gran looked stricken. She quickly withdrew her arms from the table to put her hands in her lap. "I . . . couldn't you come here for Thanksgiving instead?"

In the silence that followed, Arden stared down through the clear brown liquid at the cloves lying on the bottom of her cup.

"Oh, never mind," Gran said. "Of course, you can't. This will be your last Thanksgiving in Haverlee. Yes—I'll come."

Her sensitivity took Arden by surprise. She felt toward Gran one of those sudden surges of affection that came so rarely now, and with it a recollection of what Gran was really like, under all her busyness.

"But would it be all right if I came with Hill on Wednesday instead?" Gran went on, apparently unaware that she was the only person talking. "That way I . . . well, I have some business matters to attend to."

"Well . . ." Dad began. He glanced at Hill, who nodded ever so slightly. "Yes, I think that's a good idea. That is, if you're not afraid of riding with a reckless teenaged driver."

"Why, Tom—be ashamed! Hill is a wonderful driver!" Gran

said indignantly, then realized Dad was teasing. "Oh, pshaw—you're just like your dad—always pulling someone's leg!"

All of them laughed, especially Hill.

Arden couldn't remember living through a gloomier Thanksgiving. The weather was as bleak as a North Carolina November could offer, damp and gray with a sharp wind blowing. Although the dinner smelled and tasted as delicious as ever, the family's sadness about Big Dad pervaded the house. The table set for five seemed incomplete.

Gran shared Arden's bedroom for the first time. Before, when Gran and Big Dad came to visit, Mom and Dad had given up their bed and slept on the fold-out sofa in the living room. But now that there was only Gran, she could sleep in Arden's twin bed. Gran's things in the closet gave off a powdery, perfumed smell, like her bureau drawers in Grierson. Arden felt a bit strange about Gran's being there. Perhaps Gran felt the same way. They were very cautious and polite with each other.

At breakfast on Saturday, the day Mom and Dad planned to take Gran back to Grierson, there was an air of relief all around. Hill was to stay in Haverlee an extra day so that Arden wouldn't have to go to Grierson. She was glad to stay home, but she also felt guilty. Still, she couldn't imagine being of any use to them in the city.

"Tom, I've been thinking," Gran said suddenly, putting her coffee cup in its saucer with a little clink. When Gran said such a thing, it usually heralded something dramatic. "If you don't find an acceptable house this time around, I want you to think about moving in with me."

They all stared at her.

Mom was first to recover. "That's very generous of you,

Mother Gifford, but I'm sure we're going to find something."

"Yes," said Dad. He cleared his throat. "You know, there are lots of practical problems with that, the main one being that we have just as much stuff as you do. Your house is big, but it isn't that big."

Gran waved one hand as though to dismiss the argument. "I heard what you said last weekend, about the better homes in the better neighborhoods being out of your reach. My grandchildren need to live where they won't be ashamed to invite their friends over. It seems to me that the most practical thing is for you to move to my house for the time being."

Arden looked from Mom to Dad, wondering what they were thinking. She herself was indignant. She looked down at the table so that no one could see her anger at such a stuck-up attitude. In a flash, DorJo's words from last year came back to her, from the awful day that she had gone to the Grierson house with Arden and Dad to take Hill. *Maybe she thinks I'm not good enough to be your friend.* That's what DorJo had said about Gran, and Arden had denied it. You didn't like to think that your own grandmother was a snob. But maybe DorJo was right.

"Thanks for the offer, Mother," Dad said, "but I really think it will be best for us to find our own place, even if it's not in one of the best neighborhoods, whatever that means. We don't have to live there forever—just until we sell this house."

"Well, it's up to you, of course," Gran said, pushing her chair from the table, "but in Grierson, where a person lives makes a lot of difference."

"I think Mom and Dad are right this time, Gran," Hill spoke up. "You don't need an invasion just now."

"It's not an invasion if I invite them," Gran said.

"We don't have to decide anything right now," Dad said

briskly, as he got up from the table. "This is another day. We'll have better luck this time—I feel it in my bones."

"I hope so," Gran said, "but my offer stands in case you don't." She looked over at Arden. "Arden, would you come up and help me with my things?"

"Yes, ma'am." She gulped down half a glass of milk and quickly wiped her mouth, aware that Gran probably wouldn't think it was ladylike. It seemed odd that Gran asked her and not Hill, but maybe she was catching on to the fact that girls could carry suitcases. "Leave everything, Mom," she said over her shoulder, as she followed Gran out of the kitchen. "Hill and I will clean up after you've gone."

Upstairs, she went immediately to the bed where Gran's suitcase lay on its side, all ready to be taken down. Just as her grip closed around the handle, Gran said, "Arden, I want to speak with you before we go downstairs."

Arden tried to look surprised, but somehow she had known all along that this was coming. "Yes, ma'am?"

"First, thank you for sharing your room with me." Gran said it almost shyly. It was about the last thing Arden expected to hear.

"Oh, that's all right. I was glad for you to . . . to be in here with me." She got another grip on the suitcase handle and pulled it off the bed.

"Wait a minute, please." Now there was an edge in Gran's voice. Arden took the hint and let go of the suitcase. She sat down on the bed and gave Gran her full attention. Gran sat on the far side of the other bed.

"I hope you'll do whatever you can to convince your mother and dad that it's to the family's advantage to move to Talley Street, at least for the balance of the school year."

Arden didn't say anything. She wondered what Gran would

think if she knew that they'd already discussed the subject.

"If you live with me," Gran went on, "you'll be assigned to Brinks Junior High. It's the best in the city, one of the best in the state."

"Maybe Mom and Dad will find a house in that school district."

"They can't afford it," Gran said, shaking her head. "I couldn't buy or rent a house in that district myself if I didn't already own one. Jake and I just happened to build our house there when it wasn't such a high-priced neighborhood."

Arden felt caught. "Maybe you should be saying this to Mom and Dad."

"Oh, I will, of course." Gran rose from the bed and went over to the closet. She took down the long garment bag that held her dresses. "But I thought it would help if they knew you wanted to be in a good school."

I don't give two hoots about being in a good school! She thought it so hard that she could almost hear her voice saying the words.

Gran suddenly changed the subject. "Do you ever wear your birthday dress?"

"Well, not yet . . ."

Gran nodded as though she expected that answer. "There will be plenty of places in Grierson where you can wear it. As a matter of fact, we'll probably have to buy you another one."

Arden felt that if she didn't leave the room quickly, she would say something regrettable. She took the suitcase in one hand and draped the bag over her other arm. She left them in a chair in the hall at the bottom of the stairs and went straight to the kitchen. Mom stood at the counter writing on a large piece of paper. Arden went over and stood at her elbow, watching words about meals and chores come off the end of the pen.

74

"What is it, hon?" Mom asked, without looking up.

"I just want you to know that if Gran says I told you I wanted to move to her house so I can go to a good school, it's not true!" She spoke softly so no one but Mom would hear, but the intensity of her words made Mom turn quickly.

"Oh," she said, searching Arden's face. "All right. I'll keep that in mind." She reached out and drew Arden closer to her, smoothing her hair with one hand. "Don't worry. Moving to Gran's is the absolute last resort, so far as I'm concerned. I'm not as hot on the right neighborhood as Gran is. As a matter of fact, I'd—"

She broke off as they both heard Gran's unmistakable footsteps on the stairs. Mom let go of Arden, giving her a wink. "Don't worry," she said again.

Her confidence was contagious. When Gran came into the kitchen all ready to go, Arden wasn't angry anymore.

CHAPTER EIGHT

AS LATE AS THE NIGHT BEFORE MOVING DAY, ARDEN REHEARSED defiance in her imagination. She would stand in the empty house and shout "I'm not going!" loud enough to be heard at the end of the street. If they tried to make her go, she would cling to the newel post, wrapping her arms and legs around it. She would declare that she would rather give up the family than move to Grierson.

The problem was that, in the light of day, she found herself not only not yelling, but helping to load things into the family car and into Hill's VW. At some point, she would have to begin her open rebellion, but she kept putting it off. She couldn't tell, by looking at the faces of the others, how they felt.

Dad supervised the movers, sometimes serving as an extra hand when a large piece of furniture had to be carried. The movers were going to store most of the furniture, although Mom had insisted on taking certain pieces.

"If I have to live in that house," she had said tightly, "I want at least *some* of my own things around me."

"Even if we can hardly move around?" Dad asked.

Mom had merely glared at him, and he gave in. Now as he worked, he sweated, despite the late December chill. He was brusque with Hill and Arden. As each room was emptied of its furnishings, he made a pile of items that needed to be packed into the cars. Those were Hill's and Arden's responsibility.

As for Hill, he whistled, he made jokes, he worked quickly. He helped the movers when they needed him. He was going back to Grierson, only this time it was for good. He had cheerfully remarked at dinner the night before that at least now he wouldn't feel torn between two towns and two families. Arden, with her leaden heart, despised his cheerfulness.

Mom went about vacuuming as each room was emptied. She didn't act sad, just grim. When the movers began taking furniture out of Arden's room, she went downstairs and out the back door. She sat on the back steps and stared straight ahead. Her insides were screaming. In a little while, Mom came to the back door.

"You can go up and help Hill with the car items now," she said.

"No. I'm not going up there." She dared Mom to insist.

She heard a little sigh behind her, and then the sound of the back door closing. She stared at the yard with its bare trees and brown grass. She saw it in other seasons—in October when the late afternoon light turned leaves to gold, in spring when new green shoots like fresh salad covered every branch, in summer when the place was a mass of shade.

Her backside was sore and cold from sitting on the steps, but she couldn't bring herself to go inside again. She wondered why they were letting her get away with not helping.

Suddenly DorJo appeared from around the corner of the house. Hunched against the cold, she wore her old army surplus jacket and a gray toboggan cap pulled down over her ears. Her hands were jammed into her pockets. She came straight to the steps to sit beside Arden.

"I've been trying to get up my nerve this whole morning," she said.

"To do what?" Arden moved closer to DorJo so that they touched.

"To come over here. All the way here, I was trying to decide what I wished most—for you to be here or for you to be already gone."

"Well?"

DorJo gave her a sad little smile. "If you hadn't've still been here, I'd've sat right down on this porch and bawled my eyes out!"

They sat on, side by side. Arden's throat ached.

"I was going to come over and offer to help," DorJo said, "but then I thought that was dumb. I didn't want to make your leaving any easier. Maybe that's selfish, but it's the way I feel."

They listened to the thumps and shouts of the movers at work inside the house.

"You reckon you'll ever come back?" DorJo asked.

"Of course, I'm coming back! I'll die if I don't. And Dor, I want you to come to Grierson, too. I know what you said last year, that awful day—you said you weren't ever going there again. But you just have to now, for me. It won't be Gran's house this time—it'll be ours, too."

"I might," DorJo said. "If I can get there." She stood up and stretched, then blew on her fingers to warm them. Just at that moment, the back door opened and Mom came out. She looked very tired. Arden felt a stab of guilt. She'd been sitting here for nearly an hour, not doing anything to help.

"Hello, DorJo," Mom said. "I'm glad you're here. I have some things by the front door for you and your mother. We'll take them by on the way out of town."

"That's fine," said DorJo, "because Mama said to tell you she's made lunch for y'all. When you get ready, just come on over."

"Oh, what a nice thing for her to do!" Mom said gratefully. "But I wouldn't want her to go to a lot of trouble."

"It wasn't any trouble. I helped her."

Mom smiled. "Then tell her we accept, with thanks. It will probably be about half an hour more before we're ready to go."

DorJo turned to Arden. "Good—I guess I don't have to say goodbye yet. I'll go on home now. See you in a little bit."

Arden nodded and watched as her friend left. Mom had already gone back inside. Arden knew that she had to go in, too, and see what she dreaded most—her home, empty and echoing.

It was worse than she had imagined. Every step, every little noise, resounded in the bare rooms. Her own room, once so cozy and welcoming, was now a shell. Nothing of her was left—not a scrap. With slow steps, she walked over to her window to look out at the yard. She might as well have been peering from a stranger's window.

She went into every room, first upstairs, then down, touching the walls, trying to remember how the furniture had been arranged, how the pictures had been hung on the walls, how the light slanted in through the windows, but already her memory was confused. She hadn't paid close enough attention. She had taken for granted the way it was. As she left each room, she whispered goodbye. In her imagination, the whispers floated in the air like small gray ghosts.

Suddenly she couldn't bear being there another minute. Grabbing her few personal belongings from the bottom stair, she rushed out of the house. "I'm going to DorJo's!" she announced to anyone close enough to hear.

"Hey, wait!" Hill called after her. "We're not through!"

"I am!"

She didn't even look back. Did they really expect her to seal her own doom? At least she wasn't yelling and screaming. She wasn't wrapped around the newel post. They could be grateful for that, whether they knew it or not. But she wasn't going to make it any easier for them, that was for sure.

The cold wind made her eyes water and her nose run, which was a relief since she felt like crying anyway. She walked hard, almost marching, her sneakers thudding on the street in a kind of ragged tempo.

The smell of country ham and biscuits at the Huggins house made Arden realize for the first time how hungry she was.

"Put your stuff on my bed," DorJo ordered from the sink, where she was washing pots and pans. "Then you can come and dry these things for me."

Arden complied, glad to have something to do.

When her family arrived, and they had all finished the little awkwardnesses that people go through finding space in an unfamiliar room, they sat down at the table with its new red-and-white checked cloth. It was the first time any of the Giffords except Arden had been inside the Huggins home. Arden had a little sad feeling about that. Why had they all waited to be sociable right here at the last? This visit could have been a beginning, not an ending.

She and DorJo were the only ones not joining in the table

talk. Arden was amazed at the way her family could act as though it were just any ordinary day. The platter of ham biscuits rapidly diminished. Mrs. Huggins laughed loudly as Hill recounted the conversations he had overheard among the movers. Arden, looking around the small shabby kitchen, felt in that moment that she would gladly trade anything she possessed to still have a home in Haverlee.

Finally, Dad looked at his watch and pushed his chair away from the table. "Mrs. Huggins, we hate to eat and run, but we'd like to be in Grierson before sundown. I can't tell you how much we appreciate this."

"Yes," said Mom. "I may be able to keep my sense of humor now, thanks to your biscuits and salad."

Mrs. Huggins smiled. "We're going to miss you folks in Haverlee. I won't ever forget last year. You done a lot for me—for us—whether you realize it or not."

There was an awkward moment, and then the goodbyes began. Mom hugged Mrs. Huggins; Dad and Hill shook hands with her. They all gathered up what belonged to them except Arden. She and DorJo stood to one side, watching. Now was the time. She felt that she was about to go over a waterfall. I ought to be screaming, she thought. I ought to put my foot down. Instead, she stood close to DorJo and fought back tears.

Mom came over and held out her arms to DorJo, who moved into her embrace. "You'll have to come to Grierson to visit," Mom said. "Arden's going to be miserable without you."

A lot you care! Arden thought fiercely, staring wide-eyed at Mom so that the tears wouldn't spill over.

"She's got to come here, too," DorJo said in a muffled voice, sniffing loudly. "You got to let her come some weekend soon."

I'm not even here, thought Arden. They're talking about me like I was a statue. And indeed she did feel like one, turning to stone.

"I left my jacket and wallet in DorJo's room," she mumbled, turning away. She moved toward the little room where her jacket lay across the green chenille spread. She heard the door open and felt the rush of cool air from the outside as the others went out.

"I can't stand this," DorJo said just behind her.

"Me either," Arden said through stiff lips. She picked up the jacket and put it on, avoiding DorJo's eyes. She zipped it, felt in her pocket for the wallet, tried to think of something else she could do to put off what was coming, and failed.

"Here," DorJo said. She held out something in the palm of her hand. It was a charm for a bracelet or a key chain, a tiny silver heart. "It's to remember me by."

"Oh, Dor—it's beautiful!" Arden was stricken with remorse. "But I don't have anything for you—"

DorJo made an impatient gesture. "Real friends don't worry about paybacks. You've sure told me that a hundred times. Here—put it in your pocket."

Arden took the tiny heart from DorJo's outstretched hand. It was surprisingly heavy. Like her own heart just now. "Thanks, Dor. I'll keep it with me always."

She took the wallet out of her pocket and from it extracted her school picture. "This isn't a payback," she said, sniffling a bit. "Give me a pen."

DorJo silently handed her a ballpoint pen, and Arden wrote on the back of the picture, "To DorJo, the best friend I'll ever have. Love, Arden."

DorJo took the picture and stuck it in the frame of her bureau mirror. She took a deep breath and let it out, then she said, "Come on, your folks are waiting for you."

They walked out, arms linked, and when they came to the car, they didn't hug each other. Arden got into the back seat and closed the door. When Mom and Dad and Mrs. Huggins called goodbye, Arden and DorJo just lifted their hands and waved once. Then DorJo turned and went inside the house, and Arden stared straight ahead.

Hill had already left in the VW. Dad started the car and it began to move, away from DorJo's house, away from their own house, away from Haverlee. It picked up speed. It passed the post office, Delway's Grocery, and finally the city limits sign. Arden scarcely blinked. She was leaving for good, going into a wilderness she despised, and there was no help for it.

CHAPTER NINE

IT WAS LATE AFTERNOON WHEN THEY ARRIVED AT THE HOUSE on Talley Street. The sun, if it had been visible, would have been about to set. As it was, the day's grayness had simply deepened into an uneasy dusk. Hill's VW was already parked in the backyard.

"Well, at least we got here before the van did," Dad commented as they pulled into the driveway.

"It's a good thing," Mom said. "Can you imagine your mother's reaction to a van loaded with our furniture and no us?"

Dad was silent for a moment. He tapped his fingers on the steering wheel. "It's going to be tough, Joan—on you *and* her. The thing you have to remember is that she's coping with Dad's death as well as with our moving in."

"Don't worry," Mom said with a certain coldness. "*I* won't forget."

Arden roused to listen to this exchange. She sat up in the

back seat and looked from one to the other. "When are we going to get out?" she asked.

"Right now." Dad opened the door. "I think it would be a good idea to go in without any baggage. I'm sure Mother has ideas about where to put things, and if I know her, she'll start giving orders the minute we begin bringing stuff inside."

Arden followed Dad and Mom up the walk, keeping a distance between herself and them. She felt as though she had a large stone in her chest that weighed five hundred pounds. Dad opened the screen and turned the knob on the big front door.

"Hmmmm. Locked." He rang the doorbell and stood back. They shivered in the cold air, their breath making little puffs. In all her life, Arden never remembered having to stand and wait to be admitted into Gran's house.

"Maybe she doesn't want us," she said aloud, meaning it as a joke.

"Now, cut that out, Arden!" Dad said with unexpected heat. "Without Dad here, Mother feels she has to lock—"

The door swung open and he cut the sentence short. Warm air and light enveloped them. Gran, looking small and thin, opened her arms to them.

"For heaven's sake—I forgot I'd locked the door!" she exclaimed. "Hill came in the back way and I—Get inside, before you freeze."

In the hallway, when the door was closed behind them, remnants of the outside chill made goosebumps on Arden's legs. Hill came downstairs at that moment.

"Slowpokes!" he said, grinning. "I've been here twenty minutes."

"I was driving the speed limit," said Dad.

"Well, so was I," Hill said, looking innocent.

"All right, all right," Gran said, taking Dad and Mom by the arms and steering them toward the dining room. "I've fixed a pot of soup and some hot rolls. We're in for a long evening and we need to keep our strength up."

She assigned everyone a place to wash up, and shortly they were sitting around the table, spooning up hearty lentil soup as rapidly as they could without getting called down for bad manners.

"The movers should be here within the next hour," Dad told her. "They'll unload and place the pieces we're not storing."

"You should have had it all stored," Gran said.

Mom's shoulders straightened slightly, but she didn't say anything.

"Well, you know I asked you about that a couple of weeks ago," Dad said carefully. "You said there would be room for some of our furniture."

"Oh, well . . . maybe I did," Gran said vaguely. "But that was before I started trying to figure out where we would put everything. It's going to look terrible, you know, with furniture all jammed up."

Mom looked as if she might begin to cry. Arden was alarmed.

"The movers have already packed the things that were to be stored," Dad said, looking at his watch. "The other stuff hasn't been prepared for long-term storage. I suppose I could call and find out whether it's too late to make other arrangements, though . . ."

"That might be a good idea," Gran said. "Why don't you?"

Dad excused himself from the table to use the telephone.

"Excuse me," Mom said in a tight voice. She got up, too, and followed him from the room. Hill and Arden exchanged worried glances, but Gran didn't seem to notice.

"Well, Arden," she said, "you're getting the blue room for your very own. How do you feel about that?"

"Fine." Her voice sounded thin in her own ears.

Gran frowned slightly. "You don't sound very pleased. Would you rather have one of the other rooms?"

"No, ma'am. Really, the blue room is fine."

"Well, I know it will be strange at first," Gran said.

Arden shrugged, not able to trust herself to respond civilly. She gave Hill a pleading look.

"Arden feels fine about the room, Gran," Hill said. "She's just tired. Give her a couple of days to get her spirits back and she'll be her old self again. Right, Aardvark?"

She nodded bleakly. It was the best she could do.

"Hill, you ought not to call your sister by that silly name," Gran fussed. "It's insulting."

But I like it! Arden wanted to shout.

At that moment, Dad and Mom came back into the dining room. Mom's eyes were red. Dad looked upset.

"Well, Mother, we waited too late. There's nothing for us to do but follow the original plan."

Gran looked at Mom. "What's the matter, Joan?"

"The prospect of changing plans so late in the day threw me for a loop, that's all," Mom said quietly. "I'm all right now."

"Then I apologize," Gran said stiffly. "I suppose I should have taken more care to assess the situation." She got up from the table. "Your soup has gotten cold. Here—sit down and I'll bring you some more."

They finished the meal in glum silence except for a few pass-me-the-salt kinds of words. Arden's eyes roamed, really looking at the dining room for the first time. Besides the great oak table, it contained an antique mahogany-and-glass china cabinet, a sideboard, and extra chairs arranged around the walls. Mom's corner hutch cabinet of light maple certainly didn't fit in with this kind of Victorian furniture.

Oh, brother! Arden thought. What a mistake to come here! The moving van did not arrive. When ten o'clock had come and gone, Mom made Arden go to bed. In her weariness, she hardly remembered putting on her nightgown. She meant to stay awake, so that when the van arrived, she could get up to help unload, but the great bed and its soft comforter enveloped her in warmth. She went to sleep instantly.

In the morning, she awoke to a profound stillness. The carpets and draperies in the blue room always muffled noises from the street, but even inside the house, nothing stirred. According to the Timex, it was already nine, very late by everyone's usual habits. Quickly she got out of bed and went into the hall to listen. There wasn't a sound. She might be the only person in the house.

The upstairs hall was cluttered with items that hadn't been there when she went to bed: cardboard boxes marked BOOKS and ARDEN'S ROOM were piled on top of one another. In one corner sat her empty bookcase. She supposed that the movers had finally come in the night and that because she had been asleep, everything that belonged to her was left out here.

Discouraged, she went back into the blue room and sat on the edge of the rumpled bed, looking about with an eye to making space for her belongings. If she began to add to what was already here, it would look like a junky furniture store.

"Oh, help!" she murmured. Going over to one of the long windows, she pulled back the blue draperies and looked out. She could see the top of the summer house, its climbing vines winter-dead and brown. On this late December day, only the yard's patterns reminded her of how lovely it could be in spring and summer. All the flower beds were covered with leaves. The shrubbery and trees were bare except for a few small pines and a scrawny cedar. Her mind flew away immediately to the other window, the one in her Haverlee room, where she had watched so many seasons come and go. It seemed to her that she could see more clearly the view from that window, even though she was actually seeing this one with her real eyes.

There was a light tap on her door and, eager for company, she flew across the room to open it. There stood Hill in one of Dad's old bathrobes. He looked sleepy and disheveled, but he grinned and whispered good morning.

"Come in here!" she yelped, pulling him inside. "I was about to believe that all of you had deserted the house during the night. Where is everyone?"

"Asleep, probably, except for Gran. The movers didn't get here until after midnight. The driver said they had a bad wheel bearing and had to unload everything from the van and reload it on another. We were up until three."

"Gosh, I'm sorry," she said, remorseful. "I must've been zonked. I didn't hear anything. Why aren't *you* still asleep?"

"I woke up. Besides, I wanted to talk to you."

"Oh?" She felt suddenly wary. "What about?"

He moved to the bed and sat down. "It's going to be awful," he said.

"What is?" She could think of so many awful things, she didn't want to second-guess him.

"You folks moving in."

She was stung by the way he said "you folks," as though he and Gran were on one side and she and Mom and Dad were on the other.

"Well, it wasn't *my* idea!" she said indignantly.

"Oh, I don't mean about moving to Grierson," he said. "I'm glad of that. But it was a mistake to move to this house. If last night is any indication, there's not going to be much peace around here."

"Tell me something," she said. "If we had moved to another house, would you have gone there with us, or would you have stayed here?"

"I don't know," he answered. "I wouldn't want Gran to be here alone—at least not for a while. She misses Big Dad." He looked away and swallowed. "I do, too. But I've missed you and Mom and Dad."

She sat down beside him and leaned against him. It was impossible to stay angry at Hill. "Does Gran cry very much?" she asked.

He looked at her as though she had just come out from under a rock. "Gran? Are you kidding? She's the original stoic."

"I don't know what that means."

"Stoicism. Greek school of philosophy founded by Zeno. Stoics practiced getting rid of feelings of any kind—or at least *showing* their feelings. The thing is, Gran feels plenty—you can tell it when you look at her eyes. But in front of other people, she hides it as much as she can. I haven't actually seen her cry since the day of the funeral, although I've seen her with red eyes a few times." Hill's expression was grave. "That's what bothers me about all of us being here. She has even less privacy now. She'll hold back the feelings more than ever."

Arden hadn't thought of that. She looked at Hill with new respect. "I see what you mean. With us around, she'll be like a prisoner in her own house."

"In a way," Hill said.

"Well, what can we do?"

"I don't know—just understand what she's going through, I guess."

"Gran makes me mad sometimes," she confessed, looking down at her hands. "But I'll try to understand."

90

"Good for you!" Hill put an arm around her shoulders and squeezed. "If you get really mad, come to me to blow off steam. It might help."

Her stomach growled loudly at that moment, and they both laughed.

"Come on," Hill said, pulling her to her feet. "We'd better go get you some breakfast before your stomach wakes Mom and Dad!"

The aroma of bacon and coffee met them as soon as they stepped into the hall. "Gran's up," Hill announced, rubbing his stomach. "Hope she doesn't mind my eating in my bathrobe."

As they went downstairs together, Arden felt better than she had in days. It was good to be close to Hill again. It was the only good thing she could think of about coming to Grierson.

In the kitchen, she went promptly and kissed Gran's soft cheek.

"'Morning, Gran! It smells super in here."

"Thank you, dear." Gran was brisk. She hardly stood still long enough to receive the kiss. "Put that platter of eggs on the table, if you please. And Hill, would you get the pitcher of orange juice from the refrigerator?"

"Aren't you tired, Gran?" Arden asked. "Hill told me how late it was before everyone went to bed."

"I'm fine," said Gran. She brought the bacon and homemade biscuits to the table and surveyed the whole spread. "Now, Arden, go call your parents to breakfast."

Arden stared. "You mean . . . wake them up?"

"Well, goodness, it's going on toward ten o'clock!" Gran exclaimed. "There's a great deal to be done. This house looks as though a tornado came through."

"Yes, ma'am." Arden tried to catch Hill's eye, but he appeared to be busy at the sink and wouldn't look at her.

Mom was going to be angry, Arden thought, as she trudged upstairs. She tapped on the bedroom door. When there was no response, she opened it a tiny crack and peered in. The draperies were drawn. The two long lumps under the covers did not stir. She heard faint snoring sounds from Dad's side of the bed.

Uncertainly, she stood where she was, considering the possibility of disobeying Gran. Who would she rather have mad at her, Mom and Dad, or Gran? It boiled down to that. Things didn't look too good either way. The whole day could be ruined just on account of breakfast.

She went over and shook Dad gently. The snoring stopped, and he rolled over, squinting up at her.

"Breakfast is ready," Arden whispered. "Gran told me to wake you up."

Dad groaned and turned away from her, pulling the covers over his head. "Tell her we'll fix our own breakfast when we're ready to get up."

Arden felt a twinge of irritation. He of all people should know better than that! "She's made enough breakfast for an army," she said, not whispering this time. "She expects you and Mom to come down now. She says there's lots of work to do."

Mom's eyes opened, although they didn't focus right away. "What?" she mumbled.

Arden repeated the message.

Mom was quite awake by now. She sat up in bed and glared at Dad. "Tell Gran," she said, "that you and Hill and she should go ahead and eat. We'll be down as soon as we're presentable."

"Yes, ma'am." Arden started out, but Mom called to her.

"Remember, tell her not to wait until we get there. I can't bear it if she makes me feel guilty for cold food—"

92

"It's all right, Joan," Dad said sleepily.

"All right for *you!*"

Arden didn't wait to hear any more. She shut the door firmly and went downstairs.

"Mom says they'll be here as soon as they're presentable," she related when she returned to the kitchen. "She said to go ahead while the food's still hot." She thought that sounded better than the actual words Mom had uttered.

Gran sighed. "I would so like to get through in the kitchen at a reasonable hour."

"Mom and Dad will clean up," Arden said, slipping into her place. "That's what we do at home—we cook and clear away our own . . . things."

She caught herself on the last word. Suddenly, she realized that now *this* was home.

CHAPTER TEN

MOM DROVE UP TO THE CURB IN FRONT OF THE SCHOOL. "ARE you sure now?" she asked. "I'll go with you if you say so."

Arden shook her head because she didn't think she could say a word. Her heart felt small and dry, like an empty cicada shell. She got out of the car and slammed the door hard. As she watched it move away and re-enter the noisy line of traffic, she could not remember ever feeling so afraid.

It was a different fear from anything she had experienced before. When DorJo had disappeared last year, and when DorJo's mother had yelled at Arden and threatened to chase her, she had been afraid. But not like this. This fear was cold and steady. It would probably go on for days, perhaps for weeks and months.

She *had* wanted Mom to come with her, but somehow she knew that would be a strike against her here. Clutching her loose-leaf notebook, she gazed at the building from the edge of the school grounds, wondering which door to enter. There were many doors. Hundreds of students milled about. Probably no one was allowed inside until the bell rang. She felt like a person with a disease. She clasped the notebook to her chest and tried to make her face as expressionless as possible. A trembling began in her legs and traveled up her whole body. All around her were voices. Once in a while, she would catch a word, a phrase, a snicker, a shout, uproarious laughter. Were they talking about her? Maybe it was her clothes, or the fact that her hair was in pigtails.

She fought down panic. If she stayed out here and waited until the bell rang and everyone started to go inside, she'd probably be trampled to death. Light-headed with fear, she moved toward the nearest entrance.

A dozen or so students hung around it. Two girls chattering together eyed her and looked away indifferently. A tall black boy in a blue windbreaker stood directly by the door. He looked down at her as though he were a king and she a trespasser who had blundered into his realm.

Arden swallowed. "Excuse me . . . could you please tell me where to find the principal's office?"

Maybe she imagined that his look softened. He held the door open for her. "Come on," he said. "I'll show you."

"Aw, shit, Tyrone!" someone yelled. "You just lookin' for a 'scuse to get inside!"

"Shut up, man!" Tyrone said with a cool half-smile. "You got to be nice to people."

The laughter that erupted was cut off as the door closed behind them. "What's your name?" The boy called Tyrone asked.

"Arden Gifford."

"You from 'round here?"

"I just moved from Haverlee."

"From *where?*"

"Haverlee. It's in the eastern part of the state."

"Never heard of it," he said. His long legs put him a half step ahead of her. She walked a little faster, trying to keep up.

A red-haired woman stood in the doorway of a classroom. "Tyrone, you know you're not supposed to be in the building before the bell rings."

Tyrone stopped and made a low bow. "Miss Hart, this is a new student. I'm showin' her to the office."

The teacher made a face, half disbelief, half amusement. "I see," she said. She hardly looked at Arden. Arden felt strange. In Haverlee a teacher—any teacher—would take over the responsibility of a new student right away.

"What grade you in?" Tyrone asked as they went on down the hall. He had to bend way over to hear her answer.

"Seventh. How about you?"

"Eighth." He grinned. "Second time."

She didn't know whether to smile or not, even though he seemed pleased with himself. Where she came from, repeating a grade was no bragging matter.

"I might be there next year, too," he went on.

"That's a long time to be in one grade, isn't it?"

Tyrone shrugged. "I'm almost sixteen. I just as soon finish out here at Brinks. No need to go be one of them bottom peoples at the high school. Bunch of snots there anyhow."

"You mean you're going to quit when you're sixteen?"

"You got it." He clapped his hands together once and did a jive step. "No more pencils, no more books, no more teachers' dirty looks!" He recited the verse with a syncopated beat, accompanied by a few smoothly executed dance steps. By the time he finished, they were standing in front of a huge glassed-in space with a long counter and several inner offices.

"The office!" he announced with a flourish.

A fake-blond woman at the counter spotted Tyrone and immediately got the same look on her face that Miss Hart had.

"Tyrone Short, if Mr. Block catches you in here, he'll suspend you for the rest of January! You know that."

Tyrone was not perturbed. He held up his hands like a politician subduing a clamoring public. "Miz Gray, meet Arden . . . Arden . . ." He turned to her for help.

"Gifford," she said.

"Yeah—Gifford. She's new. I brought her down here because she never been to this place. Right now I am plannin' to go *straight* back outside. My job is done."

Mrs. Gray began to grin. She couldn't help herself. Neither could Arden. How could anyone be stern with Tyrone?

"Probably she could have found her way if you had told her how," Mrs. Gray argued, but there wasn't a lot of conviction in her voice.

"Miz Gray, you should've seen this chile out there, scared to death!" Tyrone raised his hands again, this time he was a preacher calling down bands of angels to bear witness. "When you scared, you can't remember nothin' nobody tells you."

Arden felt her face grow hot. So she had looked just the way she felt. "I really do appreciate his coming with me," she managed to say. "This is a big place."

"Okay, Tyrone, you win. Here." Mrs. Gray wrote something on a pink slip of paper. "This will get you back outside before somebody catches you. Now, go!"

Tyrone took the pink slip and bowed again.

"Thanks," Arden said to him. "A lot."

Tyrone smiled. He waved to Mrs. Gray with a spread of long fingers like a fan opening, and sauntered down the hall as though he owned the place. Mrs. Gray shook her head once and sighed, then turned her attention to Arden. "Arden Gifford. Is that right?"

"Yes, ma'am. I've just moved here from Haverlee. The principal there was supposed to send my school records."

97

"Let me check. Have a seat right there, Arden, while I look through the files."

Arden sank onto one of the black vinyl couches and waited. She watched the hands of the clock on the wall click toward 8:30. At precisely that time the bell rang, a raucous clanging that made her ears hurt. Immediately doors opened and the halls filled with scuffling, shouting, thudding, noisy students. The office area filled up. Telephones rang. People stood around waiting. Occasionally a person would sit on the couch beside Arden, but no one made any attempt to be friendly.

At 8:45 another bell rang and the office cleared miraculously. Only a few stragglers were left. Mrs. Gray smiled over the counter.

"I didn't forget you," she said to Arden, "but you can see that first thing in the morning is sort of hectic around here. I found your records. Now, if you will, just take this folder and go back here to office number 5. That's Mrs. Trout."

"Yes, ma'am." She took the folder, resisting the temptation to peek inside. Her whole school history was there, probably, including pictures of her in second grade with no front teeth.

Mrs. Trout's name was on the door, and under it the abbreviated words ASST. PRIN. Arden knocked once and someone called, "Come in!"

Mrs. Trout sat behind her desk. She looked up and smiled briskly, as though that were part of her job. "Good morning. Arden, is it?"

"Yes, ma'am." She held out the folder.

"Sit down, Arden. Let me look over what we have here and then we'll make some decision about placement."

It was quiet enough in the office for Arden to realize that her heart wasn't thumping quite so hard now. She thought about Tyrone and almost smiled. She had never met anyone quite like Tyrone.

"Your test scores are good," Mrs. Trout said, interrupting her thoughts. "I see that you were in Gifted and Talented classes in Haverlee, but I'm not sure how the level of instruction you've had compares with what the GT students here have had." She peered at Arden as though she were looking through a screen. "How do you feel about being placed in advanced classes here?"

"I don't know if I could keep up," she said. She watched Mrs. Trout write something on a piece of paper.

Mrs. Trout nodded. "The day is divided into seven periods, including lunch, and there's a fifteen-minute homeroom period between second and third. You change classes, of course. Now, let's see, you'll need a locker and a homeroom assignment . . ." Mrs. Trout sort of hummed to herself as she worked out the problem. Arden felt panic again.

Six classes and lunch. Seven different places to find. They would expect her to be able to know where she was supposed to be. Folks here didn't take you by the hand and lead you around.

"I'll take you to math and introduce you to the teacher," Mrs. Trout said. "After that, you can ask directions to your other classes. When you go to a class, go straight to the teacher and introduce yourself. I'll be in touch with them later, okay?"

She gave Arden her brisk smile again, as if to say, Didn't I do that efficiently?

"Yes, ma'am." Arden took the schedule in her damp hand. It had times, room numbers, and teachers' names. She felt sick. She had the impulse to walk right out of this office into the street and go home. Instead, she followed Mrs. Trout down the hall toward room 104, math, Mr. Wills.

"Do you have anyone to go to lunch with?" asked the girl in the desk across the aisle, as the bell rang for science class to be over. She looked older than the other seventh graders. Her soft rounded face was motherly. Her brown hair was pulled back into one large, glossy braid.

"No, I don't," Arden said, hoping she didn't sound too eager.

"Come on, then," said the girl with a quick smile. "I'm Faye Pitano. The cafeteria's such a madhouse, it can be pretty confusing."

Arden followed her gladly. During most of science class, she had worried about lunch. Hungry though she was, she had decided not to eat rather than face the crowd and noise of a strange cafeteria alone.

"I really appreciate this," she said.

Faye was sympathetic. "It's no fun being the new person. I know."

"Are you new, too?"

"I came in September. I've had a while to get used to it."

"How long did it take?" Arden asked. "It's so different from Haverlee—I don't think I'll ever get used to it."

"It'll get better," Faye said. "Most of these kids have always lived here. They grew up together, same friends and all. They've never been outsiders, so they don't know how awful it is."

They reached the cafeteria and got into line. The clamor and confusion made talking difficult, but Arden felt easy with Faye. It was like being thrown a life preserver after treading water for hours.

When they had gotten their trays and found an empty table, they ate lunch quickly, trading facts about themselves. Faye and her mother lived in an apartment near downtown. Faye's mother was a clerk in a department store. Arden told about her family and about Haverlee, and about their reasons for

100

moving to Grierson. "You'd like Haverlee," she told Faye. "People there are a lot friendlier than here."

"Maybe we always feel that way about the place we came from," Faye said. "When you have friends, a place seems friendly. When you don't—"

She had a funny look in her eyes. "The thing is, when you move to a new town or school, you have to wait to be chosen. You don't get to do the choosing. If they don't want to know you better, you can just forget it. I've moved a lot. I know."

"I've been afraid it might be like that here," Arden confessed. "It's one reason I didn't want to come to Grierson."

"Oh, well." Faye smiled again. "I don't think you have to worry. Come on—lunch period is over in eight minutes and I have to show you where the girls' john is."

Arden got through the rest of the day on the strength of the connection she had made with Faye. She was allowed to sit out the physical education class because she didn't have a gym suit yet. The coach, a man named Woody, ran around the volleyball court yelling at the players. The more he ran, the thinner his hair became, until by the end of the period it lay in little strings that barely covered his scalp. At 2:05 when the bell rang, he ran over to where she sat on the bleachers and barked at her to bring twelve dollars for a suit next day; then he was off again before she could ask him how to get to the music room.

Chorus was the last class on her schedule. Mrs. Trout had said something about its being the only elective with room for a new student right now. Arden didn't know anything about music, but she supposed that didn't matter—apparently here at Brinks they put you where there was a space.

She found the choral room at last on the lower level. The door was just closing as she raced to get inside before the bell stopped ringing.

"I say, who have we here?" The tallest, skinniest man she had ever seen opened the door to admit her. His upper lip sported a scanty mustache. Gold-rimmed glasses rested on the bridge of his bony nose. His dark hair hung long on his neck. For a moment she thought she had stumbled on drama class by mistake.

"I'm . . . Arden Gifford," she gasped, out of breath from walking so fast. "I'm new."

"How do you do?" he said formally. "I'm Mr. Kale. What do you sing?"

"I don't know, sir."

He frowned. "Who sent you here, then?"

"Mrs. Trout," she said in a small voice. She watched his face. He was plainly irritated.

"No *wonder* Brinks Junior High has such an awful chorus!" he shouted, making dramatic gestures with his unbelievably long arms. Some of the students snickered. Arden was embarrassed. "Why does she never send me musicians?"

"Now, wait a minute, Mr. Kale," said a smooth male voice that sounded familiar to Arden. Scanning the rows of students already seated in chairs on the risers, she found the speaker: Tyrone.

When he stood, the riser made him seem even taller than he was. "Mr. Kale," he said again, *"please!* This young lady is new to Brinks. Be *sensitive* to her feelin's!"

"Tyrone, sit down and be quiet." Mr. Kale was stern, but under the sternness was good humor. "When I want your advice, I'll ask for it."

Tyrone smiled and shrugged, as if to say he had done his best. Then he sat down. She smiled back at him. His intervention on her behalf gave her courage.

"I'm sorry," she said to Mr. Kale. "I'm not tone-deaf, if that helps."

102

"It definitely does," he said drily. "I don't suppose you read music?"

She shook her head. "No, sir."

"Mr. Kale?" This time it was a female voice. There was Faye, waving her hand in the air! Arden's heart leaped with pure gladness.

"Why don't you let her sit here with me?" Faye said. "She can learn the soprano part."

"Good idea." Mr. Kale looked down at Arden. "That's Faye Pitano. Fine singer. Go sit beside her. What did you say your name was?"

"Arden Gifford." She hesitated, then added, "Maybe if you'll speak with Mrs. Trout, she'll change her mind and send you a musician instead."

A faint smile flickered at the corner of Mr. Kale's mouth. As she turned to climb the riser, she thought she heard him mutter something about Mrs. Trout not knowing a musician from a muscadine, but perhaps she misunderstood.

"I didn't even *think* about you being in the chorus!" Faye whispered excitedly, patting the seat beside her. "There aren't very many of us seventh graders in it. I'm so glad you're here."

"Me, too—I think." Arden put her burden of books on the floor of the riser and sat down. "At least I'm glad you're here . . . and Tyrone."

"How do you know Tyrone?"

Arden explained quickly how he had escorted her to the office that morning, courting trouble for himself all the way.

"That's Tyrone, all right," Faye said, grinning. "Sometimes Mr. Kale gets so provoked at him he—"

"Quiet, please!" Mr. Kale rapped with a thin little stick on the side of his music stand and lifted his arms. "We're going to begin warming up."

Arden saw that as the students sang, they sat forward on the edges of their chairs with both feet on the floor and backs straight. She did, too. Once she got over her uneasiness, she began to enjoy the sound they made together. She couldn't hear her own voice, but that was all right. It seemed to her that all the voices were hers.

After a few minutes, Mr. Kale called, "Folders, please. We'll begin with the Bach. Arden, you look on with Faye today."

She moved her chair so that she could see the piece of music Faye held. It was like a foreign language to her, the notes with their flags and dots. Maybe if she heard the melody enough, she could catch on.

The student accompanist played an introduction and the chorus began to sing. Arden recognized it as a hymn tune she had heard at Gran's church. As she sang along with the others, she noticed that the notes moved up and down with the tune. Well, of course! she thought in wonderment. That must be the whole idea—notes were just a way to let you know when to go up and down. Overcome with the discovery, she almost forgot that she didn't know what she was doing.

When they came to the end, Mr. Kale continued to hold up his arms. As long as he did that, the chorus held the last note. Then, as he did a little closing twist with his hand, the sound quit, exactly as if he had turned off a radio with a dial.

"You boys have to work on tone," he said. "Let's try that part again." He rapped on the music stand and the boys sang. Arden looked around to see whose voice was so good.

It was Tyrone's. Maybe because he was in the eighth grade for the second time. His voice had already changed, unlike some of the others who were singing. Clearly, he was the leader of the boys' section.

Once the boys had practiced, the entire chorus sang the piece again. Arden felt more confident now. She began to listen—to herself, to Faye, to the whole group. Faye had a nice voice. She had no trouble hitting the highest notes. Almost before Arden knew it, the bell was ringing. A tall girl picked up all the girls' folders and Tyrone gathered the ones from the boys. People picked up their books and sat, watching Mr. Kale expectantly. He opened the door, stood back, and said, "You're dismissed. Thank you."

The class left quickly, but not in a mad scramble. Arden was impressed. Mr. Kale didn't yell or threaten, but it was the best class she had been in all day. On impulse, she paused on her way out to speak to him.

"That was fun," she said. "I don't know anything about music, but I . . . now, I think I could learn."

Mr. Kale's smile was almost joyful. "Thank you for saying so, Arden. I'm glad you're here."

"I have to run, Arden," Faye said at her elbow. "I have to catch a city bus downtown. See you tomorrow."

" 'Bye—and thanks!" Arden called after her. In spite of all the day's anxieties, there was a warm place inside her. With Faye around, tomorrow couldn't possibly be as hard.

"How'd you do today?" The sudden question startled her. She looked up to see Tyrone's lanky form looming over her.

"Well, I got through it, thanks to you and Faye." She smiled.

He seemed pleased. As they walked out of the choral room, his body moved with a rhythm halfway between a walk and a dance. "You so little," he said. "You look like you scared you gon' disappear."

"A couple of times today I think I almost did," she said. "But chorus was fun. I really liked it. And *you* have a good voice."

It was hard for Tyrone to look cool. He handled his pleasure at her praise by changing the subject.

"You goin' home now?"

"As soon as I find my locker. I haven't had time to look for it today."

"You comin' back tomorrow?"

She looked at him in astonishment. "Well, sure! What else could I do?"

He shrugged. "I don' know—stay home, maybe. Watch TV. Tell y' mama you sick."

"That doesn't work in my family," she said, shaking her head. "They already let me put off starting school three whole days."

"Well," he said, "I got to go. Maybe I'll see you tomorrow . . . if I come."

She watched him amble off, then made her way upstairs to look for the locker. The numbers of students had thinned, so she was able to find the right hall with no trouble. According to the piece of paper Mrs. Trout had given her, she would be sharing with a person named Tiffany Cell. She set all her books in a pile on the floor and tried the combination Mrs. Trout had written down. It worked the very first time. When she opened the door, though, her heart sank. The little shelf at the top held tennis shoes, a box of tissues, a dried flower. On the coat hook was a windbreaker, a pair of shorts, and a wool scarf. The bottom was piled high with books and papers. There wasn't enough room for anyone else's things.

Her first impulse was to slam the metal door as hard as she could. Her second was to cry. What she actually did was take a sheet of notebook paper and write a note to Tiffany Cells. It read:

Dear Tiffany,
My name is Arden Gifford and I'm a new student.
Mrs. Trout has assigned me to share this locker with
you. I don't know if we'll meet between classes, but

106

*I just wanted you to know whose stuff you'd be finding
in your locker after today.*

She added her homeroom number and, after a moment's
thought, threaded the note onto the lace of one of the tennis
shoes. Tiffany should see it first thing when she opened the
locker.

The pile of books seemed even heavier when Arden picked
them up again. The thought of walking the mile and a half
with such a burden did nothing to boost her spirits. Even the
hour in chorus was not enough to cancel the bone-deep weariness that settled on her as she plodded down the side stairs
and out into the street.

CHAPTER ELEVEN

ARDEN WALKED HOME MORE SLOWLY THAN USUAL, ALTHOUGH the wind whipped fiercely about her knees and the cold made her eyes water. She had just left a school pep rally—her first—and the overwhelming noise of the gym, the press of bodies, and her own feeling of being unconnected weighed on her. She hadn't known the yells today, or the names of the basketball players. It mattered little to her whether the team won or lost. She had lived here more than a month. Except for Faye and Tyrone, she was as much an outsider as she had been the first day she attended Brinks.

Was she so different now from the person she used to be? In Haverlee, she had seldom been on the outside of anything that happened, either at school or in the town. It was true that some of the people she knew had been on the fringes of things—Seth Fox, in fact, until the sixth grade when she and DorJo had discovered what a fine model car builder he was. Had Seth felt all those years the way she did now? If so, she admired him more than ever for his amiable manner. She didn't feel at all amiable.

When she reached the house, she paused for a moment at the end of the walkway to look up at it. She still felt as though they were visiting instead of living here. Its orderly white squareness seemed to keep them all on their toes. Nobody was ever relaxed anymore.

She got out her key and let herself in. Immediately the enticing smell of gingerbread greeted her. Her mouth watered as she anticipated the first bite with a glass of cold milk.

"Mom?" she called.

"Is that you, Arden?" Gran answered from the kitchen. "Your mother isn't here. Could you come here a minute, please?"

"Yes, ma'am." She was sure that her disappointment must show in her voice. Mom was the person she wanted to talk to, not Gran. Slipping her book pack from her shoulders, she left it on the bottom stair step and walked through the dining room into the kitchen. Gran stood at the sink, wiping off the last cookie sheet. Strands of hair fell over her forehead and she looked tired and very un-Granlike. On the table sat two large plates full of gingerbread squares and sugar cookies.

Arden put both hands behind her and tried not to look too hungry. At home—in Haverlee—she would have taken one without thinking, but now she felt she couldn't unless she was invited.

"Your mother has an interview," Gran said right away. "There's an opening at the county medical center."

"I hope she gets it," Arden said fervently. She went to the table and sat down. The plates of sweets were almost directly under her nose.

"Why?" asked Gran.

The question surprised Arden because she seemed really

interested in Arden's answer. "Well—because she wants a job so bad."

"But why do *you* hope she gets it?"

Arden was puzzled. "Because she wants it. It'll make her happy. Then maybe *we'll* be happier." The last sentence popped out before she realized what it would sound like. Gran hung up the dish towel and sat down opposite her.

"Have some gingerbread," she said.

"Thank you," said Arden. She reached gratefully for a piece.

"Better get a napkin first," Gran warned. "To catch the crumbs. And wash your hands—you've been handling dirty schoolbooks all day."

With a sigh, Arden obeyed, caught between laughing at Gran's predictability and being angry at her finicky ways. She poured herself a glass of milk and sat down again, waiting for Gran's next order, but Gran seemed lost in thought.

"Do you really think your mother is unhappy because she isn't working?" she asked.

"Well," said Arden, "she loved working at the Porterfield hospital. She misses it."

"I had thought it might be something else," Gran murmured, almost to herself. "The unhappiness, I mean."

Arden munched gingerbread and cast about for some response. Yes, there probably was something else—a lot of something elses.

"This is really good gingerbread," she said.

"I'm glad you like it," said Gran, straightening a little and smiling. "Did you have a good day at school?"

"No worse than usual." Arden popped the last morsel of gingerbread into her mouth and looked longingly at the sugar cookies. Maybe Gran would take the hint.

"Aren't things going well, then? Is the work too hard?"

110

Arden realized then that once again she had chosen her words poorly. "Not really—at least most of it isn't. Math is hardest, but Hill's helping me keep up."

"Then what's so bad?"

What could she tell Gran that wouldn't start a sermon? "Oh, you know—different things," she said vaguely. "It's so big. None of my teachers would know me if I sat in a different seat."

"Hmmm, well, I'm sure that's different from Haverlee," said Gran. "You may have to go up before or after class and ask questions or talk. That would help to single you out. They'd begin to know who you are."

"I don't want to be singled out."

"But in a school where each teacher has five classes a day, you have to take some responsibility in helping them get to know you."

How could she make Gran understand that she didn't want special treatment? She only wanted to be a person to her teachers, not just a body in a seat in row four. The impersonal atmosphere depressed her. She was certain that if something happened to her this very day and she was never able to go back to school, only Mr. Kale would notice.

"Have a sugar cookie," Gran said, and then before Arden could transfer the cookie from the plate to her napkin, Gran added, "I haven't seen you with any friends your own age since you came here. Maybe you'd like to have a party next week-end—invite a few girls and boys to come . . ."

"I don't think I want to do that." Arden picked up her glass and gulped the milk down in four swallows.

"You are making friends, aren't you?" Gran asked. "I mean besides Kim and Beth and Theresa—"

"They aren't my friends," Arden interrupted. "They're just people I know."

"Why, Arden—what a thing to say! Those girls have always been lovely to you."

"They've been polite, if that's what you mean. That's not the same as friends. I don't care, though."

Gran shook her head disbelievingly. "I've known those girls for so long. They're outgoing, friendly to everyone." She paused, looking closely at Arden. "I've been noticing how withdrawn you've been since you came here. If you're like that at school, I shouldn't wonder that no one wants to be around you."

Arden felt as though she had been slapped. She got up from the table. "I *do* have a couple of friends, Gran," she said, her voice on the edge of breaking. "But they don't live in one of the 'best' neighborhoods, so you probably wouldn't approve!"

She thought she could not escape from the kitchen fast enough. Gran was awful! Telling her she was "withdrawn." What a stupid word!

"Arden—"

Already in the hall, she put her hands over her ears so she couldn't hear. Just let me get my books, she thought, and I won't come out of my room until tomorrow morning.

> Box 108
> Haverlee, N.C.
> Feb. 3

Dear Arden,

You sure do write long letters. I cant write letters that long so I hope you dont expect me to but I am glad you do as I like to read them.

I try to emagine what it must be like to be there and to be scared and upset all the time, but it is hard. Everthing is so boring here sense you left that Id be glad to trade with you. Sometimes Id like to have something to be scared about just to have some exitement.

112

Mama still has her job at the nursing home. Jessie will be through at the beauty school in the spring. Granpa is doing alright but he does not feel good most of the time.

I asked Mama if I coud go and spend the weekend with you. She said we did not have the money. I told her you said you would by my ticket but she said we did not take chairity. I tried to explain to her that it was not chairity if you wanted me to come, but she can be stubbern sometimes. I will have to let it rest for a while.

Seth told me to tell you hi the next time I wrote to you. I said you woud like to get a letter from him but he turned red and said he didnt know if he woud do that. Ha!

Well that is about all the news. Like I said not alot goes on here. Write again soon.

Love,
DorJo

Arden had found the letter lying on her dresser. She snatched it up hungrily, but its brevity left her unsatisfied. She read it over three times. Finally she had to admit there wasn't much to mull over. DorJo's gifts did not include letter writing.

With a sigh, she put the letter on her desk and went over to the window. Leaning her forehead against the pane, she looked down at the brown grass and leaf-covered flowerbeds for what seemed to her the thousandth time. In Haverlee, she could never remember being bored. She hadn't even known what the word meant, really, but now she knew. It was the word for a flat, dead, gray feeling. She hadn't realized until now how much she had counted on a visit from DorJo to make life interesting again.

CHAPTER TWELVE

WHEN MISS FERREE CALLED HER NAME, ARDEN ROSE STIFFLY from her desk and walked to the front. It was the first time since she arrived at Brinks that she had stood alone before a class. Miss Ferree allowed the use of the lectern for notes, if the students did not cling to it or lean on it. Arden laid the three-by-five cards on the lectern and then quickly put her shaking hands behind her so no one would see how nervous she was.

Miss Ferree had said that when a person got up to make a speech, she should first establish good eye contact with people in the audience. Arden took a deep breath and swallowed, even though her mouth was dry. She looked around the room, searching the faces for someone who looked interested. Many students were not looking at her. One or two were going over their own speeches, looking at their notes and moving their lips. Miss Ferree sat in the back of the room. She gave Arden a smile and an encouraging nod.

"My talk today is about the town I moved from, Haverlee,"

she began in a strong, clear voice. She was glad she didn't sound as nervous as she felt. "It is about one hundred and fifty miles from Grierson in the Coastal Plain. Less than a hundred thousand years ago, it lay under the sea."

A few heads moved. More eyes focused on her. She took that as a hopeful sign.

"Haverlee is different from a city like Grierson. There are fewer people in the whole town than in the seventh-grade class at Brinks. Everyone knows everyone else's name and pretty much all about them."

There was a snicker from somewhere in the room. Miss Ferree's head turned sharply in that direction.

"Excuse me, Arden," she said, standing up. She put one hand on her hip and scowled at the class. "I need to say something about manners—about the manners of this class as an audience."

In the uncomfortable silence that followed, the other students looked at their desk tops.

"When people are speaking, you give them your attention. You look at them. You listen to what they are saying. You take into account how they feel as they stand before the class— how *you* will feel when you trade places with them. Laughter is appropriate when the speaker is saying something that is intended to make you laugh. It is *rude* when you are simply making fun."

Miss Ferree paused to let that sink in, but it was as if a hard glaze had settled over many in the room. Nothing could get in or out.

"I shall be paying attention not only to the speakers but to the audience as well," the teacher went on. "Your total grade on the project will include your behavior as an audience as well as your performance as a speaker."

At this announcement, there was a general shifting of bodies. Arden was aware of one or two fed-up glances in her direction, as though she were somehow directly responsible for the trouble they were in.

"You may resume now, Arden." Miss Ferree sat down.

Since her statement about everyone knowing everyone else's name and business had seemed so funny to someone, Arden decided not to repeat it. She proceeded rather more rapidly than was good for the speech, wanting most of all to hurry up so she could finish and escape the unfriendly atmosphere. After one or two further attempts to establish eye contact, she gave up altogether and kept her eyes on the notes lying on the lectern.

She talked about how the soil was different—dark and rich, a natural habitat for evergreens such as cedar and pine. She told stories of early settlers in the area, and how they struggled with the Indians for the land. She told about finding Indian artifacts. She talked about the friendly people and about the dozens of places to explore and play.

Finally she reached the last card:

> I have always believed that Haverlee is different, maybe because it lay under the sea for millions and millions of years. It is true that for many thousands of years it has been land, but in the whole scheme of things the land is new, still drying out. When I lived there I used to imagine that I was one of the sea creatures, and that it was dangerous for me to come too far inland away from the water. I thought I would be like a whale that is beached on the sand, and that I would die. Well, I have not died . . . yet. But no matter where else I may live, Haverlee is my true home. Someday I hope I will go back there to stay.

When she had written those words the night before, she had been pleased with them. They were how she really felt. She thought it was kind of humorous to say that she hadn't died yet. It would be all right for them to laugh at that.

But now as her eyes fell upon the words she felt sick. It was as though her bare soul lay in them. How could she say them to people who didn't care? And yet, she couldn't just stop and sit down. The speech had to have a closing. Caught between what Miss Ferree expected of her and her fear of ridicule, she hesitated a moment, trying to think of a new ending for the talk, one that was dry and impersonal and not risky at all. Her mind would not work. The words she had written on the card danced before her eyes like a happy song demanding to be sung. She opened her mouth and said them.

When she finished she dared not look at anyone. She picked up her cards from the lectern, her hands still shaking, and went straight to her seat. Her face was on fire. She slid into her desk, quickly tucking the offending cards into her notebook. Why in the world had she thought it was okay to say those things? It was the dumbest thing she had ever done. She might as well have taken all her clothes off! The stillness pervading the room let her know better than anything what an error in judgment she had made.

"Thank you, Arden," Miss Ferree said briskly. "That was very informative. Now let me make a few suggestions for the next time you make a speech."

In an impersonal tone, she listed some points for Arden to remember. Slow down. Keep your eyes on the audience. Raise your voice so that you can be heard at the back of the room.

"I was impressed with the content of your talk, and with its style," Miss Ferree finished. "Your stance was good, too— you didn't lean on the lectern and you kept your hands out of the way."

"Thank you," Arden said in a low voice.

"Now, does anyone have questions for Arden?"

Oh, dear—she had forgotten this part. Imagine, last night she had hoped for questions. Now she prayed that everyone would be silent.

"I got one," said a tall boy named Larry. He had sleepy eyes. She had thought he was not even listening to her.

"All right, Larry," said Miss Ferree. "What is it?"

"Do you still feel like if you come too far in, you'll get beached and dry out?" He didn't laugh, but he looked as though he was having a hard time not doing so.

Arden's whole body was hot. She hated Larry. She wished that she could think of an answer clever enough to jerk his head back.

"Yes," she said, clenching her fists. She looked directly into his sleepy eyes, letting him see her spite. "It's *exactly* the way I feel!"

He raised his eyebrows and shrugged, looking around at the other students as if to say, Watch out—she bites. No one else said anything. The moment dragged on, and then mercifully, Miss Ferree called on the next student to speak.

Arden kept her eyes straight ahead, but she hardly heard anything any of the students said. Instead, in her head she lived over and over the terrible mistake she had made. If only she could die or disappear; if she never had to look at any of them or speak to any of them again. She hated them. The phrase "What's done is done" popped into her head and lodged there like a bat hanging in a cave, alternately fluttering and resting.

When the bell rang for the class to be over, she deliberately lingered at her desk, taking more time than was necessary to gather her things. She pretended to search for something she had left. If she gave them plenty of time to leave, she wouldn't have to endure their hard looks or giggles.

A few students stood at Miss Ferree's desk arguing about grades, but they paid no attention to Arden. As she came out into the hall, a plump brown-eyed girl whose name was Hannah was standing by the door. She looked over at Arden and smiled.

"I just wanted to tell you—that was real pretty, what you said." Her voice had the unmistakable accent of a person from the coast. "It *is* like that, ain't it?"

And then she turned quickly and walked off in the other direction, as though, like Arden, she had learned that it was dangerous to reveal too much.

By the time Arden got to science class, something inside her had begun to harden. She felt mean. Thank goodness for Faye, who would understand and sympathize.

But Faye seemed preoccupied this morning. She sat with both elbows propped on the desk and her head resting in her hands.

"Hi!" Arden whispered, reaching across the aisle to touch her sleeve. "Are you okay?"

Faye looked up. The expression in her eyes was bleak. She shook her head. "I'll tell you at lunch," she said.

After that, Arden had trouble concentrating on science. Ms. Jones's words kept fading out. What could be the matter with Faye? Was it possible that she had had a bad experience in an earlier class, too? Maybe the school was ganging up on them. By the time the bell rang, Arden was plotting how she and Faye would conduct their own guerrilla warfare against the rest of the student body at Brinks. That's why, when Faye told her what the trouble was, she couldn't take it in.

"We're moving," Faye announced abruptly as they walked down the hall toward the cafeteria.

Arden stopped so suddenly that a boy behind her had to swerve quickly to avoid bumping into her. "What did you say?"

"Come on," Faye said. "We can't talk in the hall."

Arden stumbled along after her. Faye moving? It couldn't be. She'd been here only a few months.

They found a table in a far corner away from everyone else, and almost before they were settled in their chairs, Arden burst out, "All right now—what's this about moving?"

"It's true," Faye said. "My mother has been dating a guy she met at work—one of the assistant managers of the store. Now he's being transferred to manage the Fayetteville store and she wants to move down there, too."

"Are they getting married?"

"No. She just doesn't want him out of her sight." Faye's tone was mocking. "She's afraid she'll lose him."

Arden simply stared, trying to right herself, trying to absorb what Faye was saying. After a moment she said, "That's taking a chance, isn't it? Does he want her to go with him?"

"He hasn't said so," said Faye. "I'm pretty sure he doesn't have any idea she's moving down there. When he finds out, he's going to be mad. I think she's stupid."

Arden was startled to hear Faye say such a thing about her own mother. Maybe Mrs. Pitano *was* stupid. "That's not fair to you," she said, "making you move so she can keep a boyfriend!"

"She wouldn't see it that way." Faye seemed resigned. Arden understood a little better why her friend seemed older than she was. "She thinks she's doing me a favor, catching a husband. Then we'd have someone to support us, she says."

"Do you like him?" Arden asked.

"I've never even seen him. Mother hasn't told him about

me, either. When he comes to see her, I stay in my room with the door shut."

"But why? How could she keep her own daughter a secret?" Faye snorted. "You haven't met my mother. She's thirty years old, but she looks about twenty-three. You can see how having an almost-fourteen-year-old daughter would kind of mess up the illusion. She said that when the time comes to introduce us, she's going to tell him that I'm her younger sister who has come to live with her because our parents are dead. She's even told me to start calling her by her first name, just to get in practice."

Arden felt sick. "Faye! That's awful!"

"That doesn't half say it." Faye's whole being seemed to droop. She looked Arden in the eye. "You're the first real friend I've had in years . . . the first person I felt like I could trust. I don't love this town or this school, but having you for a friend made it all right. When I think about starting all over again in another place, it feels like being buried under a load of dirt. I'm just about too tired to dig out from under it."

Tears welled in her eyes and spilled over. "I've been to nine different schools in my life, and I'm just in the seventh grade. Sometimes I wish Mother would run off with somebody and leave me. I'd do better on my own. At least I could stay in one place and make some friends."

Arden could think of nothing comforting to say. She fished in her sweater pocket and brought out a wad of tissues, which she handed over silently. Faye's problem made her own seem of little consequence. She saw, too, for the first time what their friendship had meant to Faye. She wished she had made an effort for them to be together outside of school.

"Isn't there any way to make your mother change her mind?" Faye shook her head. "She went and found an apartment and a job there before she told me. I think she knew I'd try to talk her out of it if she didn't have everything set. The movers are coming today. We're driving to Fayetteville as soon as I get out of school this afternoon."

"This afternoon!" Arden gasped. "But . . . that means we don't even have time to say goodbye. It's not fair!"

"I guess I don't believe in fair anymore," Faye said sadly. "But I know one thing—if I ever have kids of my own, we're going to live in one town from the day they are born until they grow up and get married."

They stared at each other across the table. Arden had the terrible feeling that she had been through this before, over and over. Hill, DorJo, Haverlee, Big Dad. What was the good of getting attached, of loving anything or anyone? You were only going to lose it sooner or later.

"I don't know what I'll do without you here," she said.

"Oh, you'll be okay," said Faye. "You'll have new friends—"

"No," Arden interrupted. "I'm through with that."

Faye regarded her with puzzlement. "What do you mean?"

"I don't want any friends from here. I hate this school. The people here are snotty. I wouldn't be like them for anything in the world!"

"Arden, what's wrong? I never heard you talk like this before."

Arden wavered. She wanted so much to tell Faye what had happened that morning, but in the end she decided it would be selfish to add her troubles to the ones Faye already had, especially when they would have only one more class together before they had to say goodbye.

"Don't worry about it," she said, getting up from the table and gathering her belongings. "Come on—we have a few minutes before the bell rings. I have to get your new address so I can write to you."

She moved through the rest of the school day like someone in a trance. Coach Woody yelled at her in PE for not paying attention. She gave him a look, letting him know with her eyes that she didn't care what he thought. It gave her some satisfaction to see his surprise. He didn't expect that sort of thing from her.

She arrived at chorus a few minutes before the bell rang. Faye hadn't come in yet. Arden went straight to Mr. Kale, who was bent over the files picking out music for the class.

"Mr. Kale, excuse me."

He straightened his lanky body and she thought how like a grasshopper he was. "Yes, Arden?"

"I thought you'd want to know—Faye is moving today."

"Faye?" He frowned. "Isn't that rather sudden?"

"Yes, it is. She didn't know herself until last night."

The frown deepened. "Is she glad about the move?"

"No, sir. She's pretty upset."

Mr. Kale nodded. "Thanks for telling me. I'll speak to her."

Tyrone ambled in about the time Arden sat down. Mr. Kale said something to him, gave him some money from his wallet, and wrote out a pink slip. Arden watched the pantomime with mild curiosity. As Tyrone left again, she wondered what sort of trouble he had gotten himself into this time.

Faye was late for the first time since Arden had been in the chorus. Mr. Kale had to open the door for her.

"I'm sorry," she said. Her cheeks were pink and she looked as though she had been running. "I . . . had to stay late in math."

"It's all right," said Mr. Kale. "Have a seat and we'll get started."

"Tyrone ain't here!" called one of the boys from the back row.

"Tyrone *isn't* here," Mr. Kale corrected frostily. "I'm aware of that, thank you. Sit up, please, everyone!"

Sagging spines straightened. Legs uncrossed. In a matter of seconds, the choral class was poised, waiting to sing.

"C Major chord, Mary," he said to the accompanist. "Warm up on do-mi-sol-mi-do."

Out of the corner of her eye, Arden watched Faye to see if she could gauge her friend's mood. But Faye sang as heartily as ever. Maybe singing was the best way to keep from thinking about her troubles.

They finished warming up and had just begun sight-reading a new piece of music when there was a light tap on the door. Ordinarily Mr. Kale pretended to go berserk when anyone interrupted class, but not this time. He went over and opened the door himself. In came Tyrone, pushing before him a cart loaded with cookies, chips, several bottles of pop, some paper cups, and a container of ice.

A murmur went around the room, not too loud, though. No one wanted to risk Mr. Kale's wrath. This looked like a party, but Mr. Kale was not a party person.

"Ladies and gentlemen," said Mr. Kale with just the faintest suspicion of a smile behind the mustache, "one of our number is moving away today, and I thought it might be nice if we took a break to say goodbye. We're not celebrating her leaving, but we really should celebrate her fine singing and her contribution to our soprano section. Faye, why don't you come to the front and be hostess?"

Arden thought Faye might faint. First she turned red, then she turned pale. "How'd he know?" she asked, turning toward Arden.

"I told him," Arden confessed. "Did I do wrong?"

Faye shook her head, unable to talk. She squeezed Arden's hand once and then descended the risers. Arden hoped Faye wouldn't cry because that would make *her* cry, and she thought that once she started, she wouldn't be able to stop for months.

Mr. Kale actually hugged Faye right there in front of them all, and then he called a person from each section to help distribute the food and drink. The choral class became noisy and boisterous. Mr. Kale did not call them to order. At last, when everyone had been served, he played a chord on the piano to get their attention.

"Maybe some of you would like to tell Faye what's been good about having her here as a member of our chorus," he said. "Raise your hands if you would, and I'll call on you."

Several hands went up right away. One by one, their owners called out compliments.

"You're the best soprano we've got," one girl, a ninth grader, said mournfully. "You *never* hit a wrong note. *Now* who will we follow?"

"I don't think you ever missed a day in chorus," said one of the boys. "At least not when I've been here. That's devotion, man!"

"You've been our cheerfullest person," said a girl. "If I was feeling low when I came in, all I had to do was look at you and I started feeling better right away."

On and on they went. Arden was amazed. The speakers seemed sincere, and Faye fairly glowed under the shower of praise. Finally Tyrone raised his hand.

"I would like to speak, please," he said in his grandest manner, rising to his full height.

Mr. Kale's eyes twinkled. "Go ahead, Tyrone, but remember, it's only twenty minutes until school is out."

Everyone laughed. Tyrone acknowledged the warning with a slight bow, then he began speaking in measured overstatement, like a preacher before a congregation. "Fellow classmates, I want to speak about what Faye Pitano has meant to

125

Brinks outside of this choral room. She hasn't been in the school as long as some of us—" At this there was a snicker around the room. Most everyone knew how long Tyrone had been at Brinks. "—but in the short time that she *has* been here, she has showed the rest of us the importance of being friendly, of looking out for the peoples who fall through the cracks."

Tyrone looked directly at Arden as he said the words. She felt her face burn, and she looked away.

"Furthermore, she has been herself. Far as I can tell, she's been the same person from the first day she came here to now. Nothin' about her is phony. True, she can sing good and she knows her music, but that's nothin' to the fact that her very life is a song. Faye, we will miss you at Brinks Junior High."

Tyrone bowed again and sat, to resounding applause. Faye really was crying now, but she was smiling, too. She wiped at her eyes with the back of her hand and Mr. Kale handed her his handkerchief.

"Would you like to say anything?" he asked kindly when the noise had died down. "You don't have to, but perhaps—"

Faye nodded. She swallowed hard, and Arden found herself clasping her own hands tightly together, feeling in her throat the lump she knew must be in Faye's.

"This might be the best day of my life," Faye finally managed to say shakily. "It's the worst, too, having to leave you all, but I'll think about all the things you've said. See, I was really down—I thought maybe I couldn't start all over again in a new place. But after what you said, I think maybe I can. Maybe I'm good at it. Thank you all a whole lot."

Mr. Kale didn't try to shush the cheers and clapping with which the class responded to Faye's words. He let them go on, and then they just had time to clean up the remains of the party before the bell rang. Arden decided she loved Mr.

Kale. One day when she was able to talk about it, she intended to thank him for what he had done for Faye.

"My mother is probably waiting for me out in the parking lot," Faye said, turning to Arden at last. "You want to come and meet her?"

Arden shook her head. "I might yell at her," she confessed. "I'll just tell you goodbye here. And write. I want to know what you're doing in Fayetteville."

"Okay." Faye nodded. "You do the same. And Arden— don't get too tough. There are people here at Brinks who need you for a friend, like I did. Watch for them."

Arden didn't say anything. They hugged each other and then she watched as Faye went out the side door toward the parking lot. It had begun to rain, a cold gray drizzle blown about by gusts of wind. Arden's throat ached, but her eyes were dry. Sorrowfully, she turned to go upstairs to her locker. The walk home in the rain was going to seem hours long.

CHAPTER THIRTEEN

THE DOCTOR SAID SHE GOT THE FLU BECAUSE IT WAS GOING around, but that walking home in the rain in thirty-five-degree temperature hadn't helped. Whatever the cause, Arden found herself sick in bed for the first time since she was a little girl. The very hairs on her arms ached. Her body felt weak and trembly. Nothing was interesting, not even books Mom brought from the library. Mostly she lay with her eyes shut in a semi-darkened room, dozing and dreaming fitfully. Sometimes she felt cold even with two blankets tucked around her. Other times she thought she was frying. She coughed until her ribs were sore.

After three days of this, she awoke one afternoon to see Mom sitting on the side of the bed looking at her intently.

"Feeling any better?" she asked, putting a cool hand on Arden's forehead.

"Mmmph," said Arden, shutting her eyes again. She lay still so the coughing wouldn't start again. "Maybe."

128

"It's been a long time since you were this sick," Mom said. "You've always been the healthiest member of the family."

Arden didn't have the energy to comment. Maybe it was time for her to be sick. In some ways it was better than being well. Brinks Junior High seemed light-years away. She didn't care if she never went back. The other members of the family lived beyond her closed door. They took turns bringing juice, medicine, and soup, but she didn't encourage their staying to chat. They could talk if they wanted to, but they needn't expect her to answer.

"Tyrone called last night to see how you were," Mom said.

Her eyes flickered open again. Tyrone?

"He says you should hurry back. With you and Faye both gone, the sopranos are, as he says, 'floundering.' "

Arden managed a smile at that, imagining the girls in the soprano section flopping about like fish. "I don't suppose I'll be singing for a long time," she said in a voice that was little more than a murmur. "I can't even talk."

"In a few days, you'll have your old spunk again," Mom said.

Arden listened disinterestedly. Maybe this was what it was like when a person was dying and you told them they'd be up in no time. They probably didn't care whether they got well. She didn't. It would only mean going back to school, facing the people she didn't like, having to catch up on all the work she had missed.

"I've been thinking," Mom went on, "that it's high time you went back to visit DorJo in Haverlee. As soon as you're on your feet and can get rid of that cough, you should make plans."

Arden got very still inside. Haverlee was almost like a dream now—a good dream of a place that was bathed in soft light and held warm memories. She was often homesick, but like someone exiled to a far country, she had lost hope that she would actually see it again.

"When?" she asked.

Mom shrugged. "Depends on how soon you get well. I'd say four weeks, if you take good care of yourself. The weather should be improving, too. It'll be near the end of March by then. Your dad and I will talk it over. Maybe he can drive you down on Friday and bring you back on Sunday." She patted Arden's arm. "Anyway, we can work out the details later. Ready for your medicine?"

Arden grimaced. The pills she had to take were very large and hard to swallow. Once she had held one in her mouth too long and its bitterness made her gag. "I sure will be glad when I'm through taking these," she grumped, pushing herself upright so she could swallow the juice Mom handed her with the pill.

"So will I," Mom said. "It will mean you're almost well."

After Mom went out, Arden lay there thinking. Her mind had waked up and did not seem to want to drowse anymore. She imagined herself traveling along the highway leading back to Haverlee—the evergreens, the flat terrain, the creeks and rivers, the particular smell of watery things, and finally Haverlee itself set like a small jewel among fields and groves of trees. The familiar ache of longing stirred in her, at once sweet and bitter. She had to admit to herself that she did want to get well enough to go back to Haverlee, even if it cost her the freedom she had right now from Brinks Junior High.

As Mom drove up in front of the school, Arden had a flashback to the day in January when she had first come here. At least today, she wasn't scared.

"Now, if you start to feel bad, call me," Mom said. "And

here's your absentee excuse." She handed over a folded piece of paper. "I've told them you've had a bad case of flu and that I don't want you to participate in PE for a while. I've also told them that I don't want you to stay all day if you feel bad."

"I'm okay." Arden already felt weary. Just managing to sit upright at a desk all day would be hard.

"And if you don't feel like walking home this afternoon, call me. I can be here in fifteen minutes."

"Okay." As Arden reached for the door handle, Mom quickly leaned over and kissed her cheek.

"Take care now," she said. "You have to get well for Haverlee."

The phrase sang inside her head as she walked the few steps to the front entrance in the chilly air. It lifted her spirits a little. The usual crowds of students hung around waiting for the bell, but now many of the faces had names. Today, instead of being scared, she was merely indifferent. Heading straight to the front door, she opened it without thinking.

"Hey, wait—you can't go in there till the bell rings!"

The rough voice startled her so that she let go of the door handle. In the next moment, the speaker planted himself between her and the door. He was at least a foot taller than she. He wore a navy toboggan cap over his ears and an army fatigue jacket. She didn't know him, but the name ROGER SMALL was printed in large block letters on the notebook piled with other books near his feet.

"I have an excuse," she said. It was strange that she wasn't afraid, only angry. She reached around him for the door handle.

"You ain't going in!" He pushed her hand away. "Nobody goes in till the bell rings. That's the rule, little seventh grader."

She went rigid with anger. "I *am* going in, too!" she said, raising her voice as much as she was able. "And if you don't get out of the way, it's going to be too bad when I get to the office and report you."

"Aw, you don't even know my name," he taunted.

"Oh, is that so, Roger Small," she shot back. She noted with satisfaction his shocked surprise. He moved then, but as the door closed behind her, she heard him mutter something obscene.

She coughed all the way to the principal's office.

"Heavens!" Mrs. Gray said with alarm. "Are you all right?"

"Not very." Arden leaned on the office counter and fished from her jacket pocket the note Mom had written. "I've had the flu."

"Sit down over there. I'll get you some water." Mrs. Gray fetched the water in a little paper cup, then read the note and filled out a white slip for Arden to take to all her classes. "You don't look as though you feel well," she said. "Maybe you came back to school too soon."

Arden almost laughed. Even if she'd waited until May to return, it would've been too soon. Maybe Mrs. Gray wouldn't think that was funny.

She ate lunch alone in the cafeteria after science class. She missed Faye terribly. The thought of eating alone for the rest of the school year was almost unbearable. Maybe she would start skipping lunch and get a library pass.

By last period, she felt so tired and discouraged that even Mr. Kale's hearty welcome back to choral class didn't boost her spirits much. Unable to sing, she followed the music with her eyes. She imagined that she could hear Faye's voice singing strongly among the sopranos. She wondered if Faye was singing at the new school.

As soon as the final bell rang, Tyrone stepped down to her

side from the riser above. "Glad you back," he said, "even if you *do* look like you been in a prison camp."

She smiled weakly. It was impossible to be insulted by Tyrone, especially when he told the truth. "I can't say I'm glad to be here, but thanks anyway for missing me. I appreciated the call."

"With you sick and Faye gone, the sopranos been soundin' like a chicken yard after a tornado," he commented. "Mr. Kale looked some kinda relieved when you walked in today."

"Well, I'm no use to him as long as I can't sing." She sighed. "I'm never going to catch up on all I've missed."

As they passed Mr. Kale to go out, he said, "Take care of that throat, Arden. Don't try to sing until you're absolutely well."

"Yes, sir. Don't worry—I couldn't if I tried."

Instead of going his own way, Tyrone stayed with her. "You walkin' home this afternoon?"

"Planning to, after I go to my locker," she said.

"I'll walk with you," he said. "In case those books gets too heavy."

She felt so grateful she almost cried. Gosh, she thought, as they climbed the stairs, I must be in really bad shape!

At the top of the stairs, she saw that Tiffany was already at the locker, leaning against its door and gazing up into the eyes of a tall boy who Arden decided must be a ninth grader.

"Love birds," Tyrone said drily, under his breath. "You might have to set off a firecracker to get 'em to move."

Arden hoped they'd hear her coming and leave, but they were like people in a trance. She was going to have to go right up to them and interrupt. She took a deep breath and said, "Excuse me. Could I get to the locker, please?"

Slowly, very slowly, Tiffany's blue eyes left off adoring the boy and swiveled in Arden's direction. The eyes were ringed with liner, mascara, and bluish shadow. Her abundant hair was styled to look as though she had just gotten out of bed. Arden felt, in her presence, like a piece of notebook paper— flat and colorless, with a few pale lines.

"Sure," Tiffany said. She took the boy's arm and moved him slightly to one side. Arden found that when she opened the door it rested against Tiffany's arm. She shot Tyrone a despairing look, but he was choosing to look in another direction. He whistled a tuneless tune, jingled some coins in his pocket, and waited for her to finish.

"Where've you been?" Tiffany said.

At first Arden wasn't sure if the question was meant for her, but the eyes looked at her and so she answered.

"Home. Sick. I've had the flu."

"Oh. I thought maybe you'd quit school or something."

Arden put a couple of books on the shelf and shoved a notebook and her math book into her book pack. "No," she said.

"Sure was nice, having the whole locker to myself," Tiffany went on. She was smiling.

"I'll bet," Arden answered. "Sorry to disappoint you by coming back." She slammed the locker door and turned away.

Neither she nor Tyrone spoke until they were on their way downstairs again. "Whew!" he said. "I thought you was gon' slap her up side the head!"

"She's taller than I am," said Arden.

Tyrone shouted with laughter, but when she didn't join in, he sobered up. "Don't let Tiffany get to you," he said. "She didn't mean it like you took it. Actually, it was sort of friendly teasin'."

"I don't tease so well these days," she said grimly, as they went through the heavy doors to the outside. The afternoon was pleasant, with lots of sun and very little wind. Something about it suggested that spring might not be long in coming. Maybe she could hold on, if spring came soon.

"Arden! Wait a minute, will you?" someone called. The next minute Kim came running up, clutching three large pieces of posterboard under one arm and holding a handful of colored felt pens.

"You're just the person I wanted to see!" she bubbled, flashing an easy smile which took in Arden and Tyrone at the same time. "The Pep Club is looking for people to make publicity posters for the Friday game. We want the whole student body to be there. Would you do one for us—please?"

"I can't," said Arden. "This is my first day back in nearly two weeks. I have too much work to catch up on."

"Oh, come on, Arden," Kim wheedled. She flashed the smile again. "It would only take a half hour."

"No, I can't."

Kim's smile began to fade. "We really need everyone's cooperation, Arden. The team is number one. We want 'em to stay on top. They need our support."

"I'm *sorry*, Kim—I've told you I can't!" Arden felt the dreaded tickle in her throat that signaled the onset of a coughing spell. She began walking away, full of fury. Let Kim pick on the patriots, the ones with the school spirit. She, Arden, wouldn't cheer for Brinks no matter *which* team they played!

Tyrone had stayed behind when she walked away. Now he came trotting up, holding one of the pieces of posterboard. A red felt pen was balanced precariously behind one ear.

"Did I embarrass you?" she said gruffly.

"Nope," he said. "I told her how bad off you been. Then she said why didn't I do one, and I said 'cause she never asked me. So now I'm doin' one."

"I bet she won't ask me to do anything else anytime soon," she said.

"You prob'ly right," he allowed. "Look, Arden, these peoples didn't do nothin' to you. What you want to act mean for? Whatever you mad about ain't they fault."

Tears stung her eyes. "Who says I'm mad?"

"I know mad when I see mad," Tyrone said. "I been mad myself. You won't get no sympathy bitin' heads off."

"I never asked for sympathy!" she said fiercely.

Her vehemence silenced him for a moment. "Here," he said, reaching for her book pack. "Gimme that thing."

"I can carry it," she protested, but he was already slipping it from her shoulders and adjusting the straps. He handed her the floppy posterboard he'd gotten from Kim.

"Don't you see how phony Kim is?" she said. "She's using you to get something done. She doesn't care about you."

"What's that got to do with anything?" he said. "I want to make a poster. I'm good at it."

It was her turn to be silent. The taps on Tyrone's shoes clicked pleasantly on the cement sidewalk. Finally, she said, "There's no way I can make you understand—everybody wants to be *your* friend. Everybody likes you."

"That ain't so," he said. "Some peoples just like to have me around 'cause I'm good for a laugh. But I tell you what— if anybody's down on me, they got to have they own reasons. I ain't givin' 'em any."

He turned his head to look at her as they walked along. "You givin' people reasons right and left, and you too good for that. When you first showed up at Brinks, I said to myself this person different—she got class. Now you go around frownin' all the time, talk bad about the school, don't join in anythin'. Ain't no point in it. You the person gets hurt."

136

"You preach a lot," she grumbled.

Instead of taking offense, he laughed. "Maybe that's what a person have to do—preach. Nobody ever said anybody have to listen."

"Things are different in Haverlee," she said, staring off down the street, thinking of herself in that peaceful place where she could be her true self once again. If Tyrone could see her there, he would hardly believe it was the same person. "I'm going back there."

"You mean, to stay?"

She was going to answer "to visit," but instead she said, "Maybe." The idea filled her with a strange excitement. What if she *did* push Mom and Dad to let her stay?

Tyrone frowned. "You sound like you serious."

"I am." She nodded emphatically, more for her own benefit than for his. She had never asked her parents for anything important. She had always done what they expected of her. Maybe it was time to claim what was due her.

"What would it take," he asked, "to get you to change you mind?"

She turned her head to look at him. He wasn't teasing. "I . . . nothing. Nothing could get me to change my mind. I want to go back."

"You got a chorus to sing in down there?"

"No—but so what? There are other things to do."

"You a good singer. You keep on, you'd be really good by the time you get to high school."

She felt a pang, but pushed it aside. Chorus was satisfying, but it was just one thing. It wasn't enough. "I want to go back," she said again.

"Well," he said with a sigh, "I don't know nothin' else to say."

They were almost at the corner. "This is where I turn," she said, handing him the posterboard. "I'll take the book pack now."

The pack's sudden weight surprised her. "Thanks for carrying it for me," she said. "I'm not sure I could've made it the whole distance."

" 'Welcome," he mumbled. "Guess I'll see you in school tomorrow."

"Yes, sure," she said.

"When you goin'?"

At first she thought he meant to school, then she realized he was still thinking about Haverlee. "As soon as I get well. Probably three or four weeks."

"Okay," he said, smiling a little. " 'Bye."

As he turned away, she wondered why he smiled.

CHAPTER FOURTEEN

DINNER WAS OVER AND THE DISHES WERE DRAINING IN THE SINK. In the living room, Mom lay on the sofa, reading. Dad was looking at the evening paper, hinting that he'd like to go to a movie if a certain nice-looking woman would be his date. Gran had her photo album open on the card table and was placing some new pictures in it. The placid scene made Arden furious. They were all so satisfied.

"I have something to say," she announced. Mom, Dad, and Gran all looked up at once, as though their heads were on a common string. Dad lowered the newspaper with a soft, crumpling sound. Mom stuck one finger in the book and closed it. Gran put down the picture she had been about to place in the album and folded her hands in her lap.

Having everyone's attention so suddenly made her self-conscious. She had the feeling they would be laughing at her if they weren't so polite.

"I don't want to live here anymore. I want to go back to Haverlee."

Neither Dad nor Mom spoke right away. Gran made a little hmmphing noise and picked up the picture again, looking through the bottoms of her glasses to see where it should go.

"Well," said Mom, giving Dad a quick glance, "do you mind telling us why you decided this all of a sudden?"

"It's not all of a sudden," Arden said. "I hate it here. When I went back to school today, I remembered again how much I hate it."

"I didn't know you hated it," said Dad. "I thought things were getting better. I never heard you complain."

"What good would that have done?" she said. "You would just say I was being unreasonable."

Dad tried another tack. "How would going to Haverlee change things?"

"I wouldn't dread getting up every morning the way I do now."

A long silence greeted her words. Gran pursed her lips, but she didn't say anything.

"We talked about this before, Bird," Dad said, "before we left Haverlee. You know your mother and I would miss you a lot."

Arden looked at him coldly. "You missed Hill, too, but you let him come to Grierson when he wanted to."

"He had grandparents to live with," Dad said. "Don't you remember when he and I talked at the beginning? He knew he couldn't come to Grierson unless Gran and Big Dad took him in."

"Well, it's not *my* fault we don't have kinfolks in Haverlee," she said hotly. "Friends can be just as good as relatives. Mrs. Huggins would let me stay with her and DorJo."

"Do you know that for a fact?" Dad asked. "I don't remember her making such an offer."

"Only because I didn't ask her to," Arden said. "Then, I

140

couldn't imagine being away from . . . from my family. Now I—" She had been about to say, Now I don't care, but she caught herself in time. It sounded harsher than she meant. "Now I could do it."

"I don't know what to say," Mom said after a moment. "I can give you all our reasons against. You should be with your own family. The schools are better here. Mrs. Huggins has enough to worry about without adding another responsibility. Besides, she and DorJo live in very cramped quarters." She stopped and took a deep breath. "But I'm sure you could argue the other side of every one of those reasons. As far as I'm concerned, it boils down to one answer—it doesn't feel right to me to let you go back."

"Nor to me," Dad chimed in.

"That's the dumbest reason I ever heard!" Arden said.

"I wish you'd give Grierson a fair chance," he said, as though she hadn't spoken. "I wish you hadn't made up your mind to hate it."

She strode across the room and stood beside the door. "You're not listening to me," she said, her voice trembling. "I feel like I'm talking to robots! One way or another, I'm going back to Haverlee for good; I don't care what you say!"

And before anyone could respond, she opened the door and slipped out, closing it quickly behind her. Let them think about *that* for a while, she thought, as she fled up the stairs to her room.

No one followed her. No one tried to reason with her. She sat at her desk and tried to study, but her thoughts kept returning to the scene downstairs. Would they punish her by taking back their promise to let her visit DorJo? She thought of Gran at the card table putting pictures in the photo album, not saying a word. She bet Gran had plenty to say after she left the room. Maybe Gran was the reason neither of her parents had come up to talk to her. The more she thought about it, the angrier she became.

Shortly she heard Mom's and Dad's voices in the downstairs hall, then the front door opening and closing. When she heard the sound of the car driving away, she concluded that they had gone to the movie after all. The house seemed to settle into an abnormal stillness. She threw down her pencil and went to the door of her room to listen.

The clinking of plates and silverware floated up faintly from the kitchen. Gran would be putting things away. She couldn't stand for dishes to sit overnight in the drain.

Arden descended the stairs, heading for the kitchen. She didn't want to talk to Gran, and yet she couldn't seem to stop herself. She made no noise crossing the darkened dining room. Somewhere in the back of her mind was the notion that she could always turn around and go back upstairs before Gran knew she was anywhere around, but she didn't. She could tell by listening exactly what Gran was doing. Cups and saucers going into the hutch. Now the silverware being tossed piece by piece into the drawer beside the sink. Arden hesitated in the doorway, blinking in the bright kitchen light. Gran turned from her task and saw her.

"Well, hello," she said pleasantly enough. "I thought you'd gone to sleep."

"It's only eight-thirty," Arden replied.

Gran nodded. She opened one of the cabinets and reached for a stack of plates.

"You think I'm acting like a baby, don't you?" Arden said defensively.

"Not at all," Gran replied. She put the stack of plates on the shelf. "More like a teenager, actually."

If Gran had slapped her she wouldn't have been more stunned.

"It's all right, though," Gran went on matter-of-factly. "You *are* a teenager."

"I don't think I act like a teenager at all," Arden protested. "I don't screech and squeal. I don't listen to a lot of loud music. I don't try to dress like everyone else, I don't—"

"Now, just a minute." Gran raised a hand. She sat down at the kitchen table and indicated that Arden should do the same. "You misunderstand me."

Reluctantly, Arden took a seat across the table from Gran.

"I'm not talking about TV teenagers," Gran said with some impatience. "You certainly aren't like that, thank goodness! But no matter how much of an individual you are, you can't escape the misery of growing up."

Arden felt like putting her hands over her ears. Instead she said rather stubbornly, "I wouldn't be miserable if some things were different."

"Such as living in Haverlee instead of here?"

She nodded.

"Well, you could be right," Gran acknowledged, "but there's no way to tell, is there? You're here and you're miserable and that's that. What I'm talking about is pulling away."

"Pulling away what?"

"Pulling away *from* your mother and father. Making your own decisions. Taking a chance at being disobedient once in a while. Doing a bit of yelling to get a point across. That's very teenaged."

Arden looked down at the table. It was humiliating to hear Gran talk about it that way.

"So you're saying Mom and Dad won't take me seriously because I'm acting the way teenagers usually act?"

"No, I'm not saying that at all. I think they take you very seriously. They want you to be happy, as much as they wanted Hill to be happy."

143

Arden kept looking at the table. "I know *you* don't think I should go back," she said tightly, "but I don't think it's fair for you to try to convince Mom and Dad."

"Now, just a minute, young lady," Gran said crisply. "I haven't said a word to your parents about this subject. Don't jump to conclusions."

Arden sighed loudly. She wondered why she kept on sitting here listening to this.

"No, on the contrary," Gran said, as though she didn't notice Arden's impatience, "I rather think they ought to let you try it, at least for the rest of the school year. It's only about three or four months until the end of school. If Mrs. . . . er . . . what's your friend's last name again?"

"Huggins."

"If Mrs. Huggins is willing for you to stay with them, I see no reason why you shouldn't."

Arden thought that perhaps something was wrong with her hearing. Gran in favor of her going back? It was scarcely to be believed.

"As I say, I haven't expressed my opinion to Tom and Joan because it's none of my business. But if I were asked, I'd tell them what I just told you."

Arden felt downright peculiar, not quite trusting. "Why?" she asked. "Why do you think it's all right for me to go back to Haverlee?"

Gran shrugged. "It will be a good test. Maybe you'll find it isn't the wonderful place you remember. Maybe you'll be relieved to come back to Grierson and your family."

Arden got up from the table. She kept her voice even, though she felt like yelling. "You're wrong," she said. "I can tell you right now you're wrong. If I ever get there, I'll never want to leave again."

For the space of a moment Gran looked at her with something like pity, which Arden hated. Then she said with another shrug, "Maybe you're right . . . I could be wrong. But I'd be willing to take the chance."

"Tell them what you think, then," said Arden. She said it like a dare.

"You still don't understand, do you?" said Gran. "If I'm asked, I'll tell them what I think. Otherwise they'll never know." She looked over the tops of her glasses. "At least, they'll never know from *me*."

The plan came to Arden that night while she lay wakeful, staring up at the darkened ceiling of the big room. Their house in Haverlee was still unoccupied. She knew exactly where the keys to it were kept—in the top drawer of Dad's dresser in a little square box full of various odds and ends of keys, paper clips, cuff links, pennies. The Nottingham Realty Company had a duplicate set, in case someone wanted to look the house over.

She would get the key to the front door—Dad would never miss it from all that junk—and take it with her when she went to visit DorJo. It wasn't perfectly clear to her what she might do with the key, but having it in her possession would give her some power over her future that she did not now have. Once she got there, she would discover how it could be used.

CHAPTER FIFTEEN

IT WAS FRIDAY, THE FIRST OFFICIAL WEEKEND OF SPRING. ARDEN stood impatiently on the walkway in front of the school waiting for Mom and Dad to pick her up, as they had promised. The sun warmed her back, even though the March wind was brisk. The silver heart DorJo had given her hung on a chain around her neck. She touched it briefly and smiled to herself. All up and down the street across from the school grounds, the yards bloomed with white and red azaleas. The soft yellow-green of new foliage had turned the drab street into a postcard picture. She had to admit that, in spring, Grierson didn't look so bad.

But perhaps any place would look beautiful today. To think that this very night she would be eating dinner in DorJo's kitchen! She hugged the thought to her, savoring it, trying not to remember that the weekend would be over in two days. The minute hand of the Timex seemed to be stuck. Even the second hand moved with wicked tedium. They should be here by now. It was almost one o'clock. Behind her, the classrooms

146

of Brinks Junior High were as busy as ever, but she felt that they had nothing to do with her. Maybe this was the way people felt when they were let out of prison.

She spotted the car as soon as it turned into the street three blocks away, and to save every possible second, she walked toward it. As it rolled to a stop at the curb, she opened the door and slid into the back seat.

"Did you bring my suitcase?" she asked right away. "I left it by the front door—"

"Your suitcase?" Dad looked shocked. "Oh, my stars! I think we forgot it! Joan, we have to go back—"

"Oh, Tom, hush!" Mom said, laughing. "Arden's in no mood for your teasing." She turned around so that she could see Arden. "Your suitcase is safely in the trunk. It was the first thing to go in."

Arden breathed deeply and leaned back, smiling. Now, she thought. Now. The key to the Haverlee house made a small hard lump in her jeans pocket. A few nights ago, she had had a dream that when she let herself into the house, all the furnishings were there, just as they used to be.

"That suitcase felt pretty heavy to me, Bird," Dad said. "What're you taking—books?"

"No," she answered, looking out the window. "Just clothes."

"You're only going to be there two days," he said. "You must've packed every garment you own."

"I didn't know what I might need," she said vaguely, but her heartbeat quickened. She knew what he was getting at. Every day for three weeks now, they had had the argument about her going back to Haverlee for good. At first Mom and Dad had been calm, but when they saw that she was serious, their arguments took on a frantic tone. Even so, they did not

147

go back on their promise to allow this visit. She knew they were nervous about what she might do. She did not say anything to relieve their anxiety.

With half an ear, she listened to Mom and Dad chattering. They were almost as excited as she was. This was their first trip away together in a long time. Hill had been invited to the mountains with some friends, and Gran would have the house to herself. The weekend had turned out well for everyone.

Arden leaned forward and rested her elbows on the back of the front seat.

"Excited?" Mom asked.

"Like you wouldn't believe," said Arden. "I never looked forward to anything as much as this."

"Well, I hope Haverlee meets your expectations," Dad said. In the rearview mirror, she could see the frown creases in his forehead.

"It will," she said with confidence. "All it has to do is be there."

"Things may have changed."

"Changed? In three months?"

"Don't you think *you've* changed in three months?" Mom asked.

"Only on the outside. As soon as I get back to Haverlee, I'll be the same as I was before I left."

Mom sighed a little. She started to say something, but then changed her mind. Arden sat back and turned her attention to the landscape. On trips from Haverlee to Grierson, when she was younger, she had tried to find the exact point where the soil changed from dark to red, where the land went from flat to hilly. She was hungry now to see the dark, flat terrain. She daydreamed of the places where she and DorJo had spent so many hours of fun—the hideout in the clay bluffs, the creek below town where the cattails grew in abundance, the woods and fields beyond.

The car seemed to creep along, but after what seemed to Arden to be a very long time, she began to see some recognizable landmarks. Certain houses, an ancient vine-covered tobacco barn, a country store, a stand of trees beside a pond. They were all familiar pictures put away and forgotten until this moment. She didn't even want to blink, for fear she would miss something.

A sign said REDUCE SPEED AHEAD.

"Slow down, Dad," Arden said.

"I'm not exceeding the speed limit," he protested.

"I know—just don't go so fast I'll miss seeing things. Please— just a *little* bit slower!"

With a sigh, Dad slowed the car. A pickup truck behind them honked its horn loudly and then passed them with an impatient roar. Arden stared after it, hoping to recognize the driver, but he sped away too quickly.

"The city limits sign is just around the curve," she said. "We're almost there!"

"Ah," said Mom, "I feel that I've hardly been away. It doesn't change at all, does it?"

"No," said Arden with a certain pride. She'd been trying to tell them that all along.

"How would you like to cruise the streets and see everything once before we take you to DorJo's?"

"Oh, Dad—that would be great!" She bounced once on the seat. "Please do!"

Dad turned into the street that went by Delway's Grocery, cruising in low gear. Some people stood in front of the post office. Arden scanned faces. Miss Betty Barnes, Tab Lucas, Henry Tanner. They all looked up as the Gifford car passed, squinting to see who it was. Arden rolled down the window and waved, calling out their names. To her surprise, the trio didn't rush gladly toward them, but smiled and waved politely. "That's funny," Arden said, as the car moved on. "They acted like they'd never seen us before!"

"Well, you have to remember they're not expecting to see us now," Mom said. "Sometimes when you're not expecting to see someone, you can't believe your own eyes."

Arden forgot her disappointment at not being recognized as they drove slowly through the streets, finally approaching their own. Everything looked as it should—the trees, the yards, the shrubbery, the flowers. It had all been sitting there waiting for her to come back.

Then at last they arrived at their very own house, with its FOR SALE sign in the front yard. Arden stared. Utterly desolate and empty, the house's windows gaped, or, where the draperies had been left, they blocked out the town. The sight shocked her. Because she had not looked back when they moved, she had never seen it like this.

"Houses need people," Dad commented. "I wish someone was living here, even if they were only renting." He turned the car into the driveway and stopped. "You know," he went on, "I should have brought the key. Maybe if we went in and walked around a little, the house would feel better."

The key burned inside Arden's pocket. Involuntarily, she reached in and grasped it. She clamped her teeth together to keep from saying, But I brought it! Right away they would want to know why. They would wonder why she sneaked the key instead of asking for it outright.

Mom turned around and looked at her. "Does it make you sad?"

Arden nodded and looked away. Her heart was pounding so hard she was sure Mom could see.

150

"Well, perhaps we shouldn't hang around here," Dad said, backing the car into the street. "Let's go on to DorJo's."

But as they started away, Arden caught sight of two familiar figures on the sidewalk. "Dad!" she shouted. "It's Nina Wall and Judy Ross! Let me out—I can walk as far as DorJo's with them."

"Well, sure, if that's what you want to do." Dad obligingly stopped to let her off at the curb. "We'll meet you at DorJo's."

She flung open the door and scrambled out before he could change his mind. In another moment, she was standing on Haverlee soil. She almost felt like kneeling down and kissing it, the way she'd seen the Pope do on TV, but there wasn't time. Nina and Judy were walking pretty fast. If she didn't hurry, she wouldn't be able to catch them.

It was funny—when she had lived here Nina Wall was one of her least favorite people, but now that she had been away, even Nina looked good. She cupped her hands around her mouth and called: "Nina! Judy! Wait for me!"

The two girls stopped and turned around. She ran toward them, her feet seeming barely to touch the ground. As she ran, she watched their faces for the moment when they would recognize who she was.

But the smiles she expected did not materialize. First she saw puzzlement, then mild surprise, and finally—even as she ran up to them—a sort of matter-of-fact acceptance of her, as though she had never really been gone.

"Well, hey!" said Judy. "How'd you get here—walk?"

"No, my folks brought me. I made 'em let me out of the car." She couldn't stop grinning, looking from one to the other. When were they going to tell her how great it was to see her? "You must be on your way home from school," she said, by way of making conversation. "How was it?"

Judy seemed baffled by the question. "You mean school? Awful, as usual."

"Yeah." Nina rolled her eyes. "Not worth talking about, specially on Friday. Say—what are you doing here, anyhow? Are y'all moving back here or something?"

"No," Arden said regretfully. "I wish we were. I just came back for the weekend to visit DorJo. I've really missed this place."

They began walking again. "Didn't you go to live in Grierson?" Judy asked.

"Yes," said Arden. She took a breath to begin telling them what Grierson was like.

"Boy! I can't imagine missing Haverlee after you've lived in Grierson where there's so much to do," Judy said. "I can't wait to get away from this town!"

"Me, either," said Nina emphatically.

Arden's heart turned over. Why was life so unjust, letting these two stay in Haverlee while she had to leave against her will? While she searched for something else to talk about, the two girls resumed the conversation they must have been having before she had called to them.

"So after Jean said that," Nina fumed, "I told her I didn't care if I ever laid eyes on her again. I'm not talking to her— I mean it!"

"Well, you'll have to *some*time," Judy replied, "long as you go to school."

"I don't either. I won't have anything to do with her, the snot!"

Arden felt that she had suddenly become invisible. She walked beside them in awkward silence, listening to chatter of events she knew nothing about, wishing she had an excuse to leave them and run ahead.

Dad's car was parked in front of DorJo's house, but that was still a block and a half away. She began to count her own steps . . . thirteen, fourteen, fifteen, sixteen. If only she had stayed in the car, she and DorJo would already be together now. What a stupid thing, to waste her precious minutes on Nina and Judy! She kept her eyes straight ahead, focusing on the car and DorJo's house.

Then a figure darted down the steps and began running toward her.

DorJo!

Arden broke into a run. They grabbed and hugged, jumped up and down, squealed and hugged some more.

"When I saw your Dad's car and you not in it—"

"I shouldn't have gotten out, but I was so glad—"

"I couldn't sit still in school—it's a wonder I didn't get sent to the office—"

"I haven't slept in two days—"

Their words tumbled and bumped. For Arden, the terrible feeling of being out of place passed like a bad dream. She was home now, in her rightful kingdom, so happy she thought she would burst. She hardly noticed when Nina and Judy walked by, she and DorJo were so wrapped up in asking and answering each other's questions.

"Well," said Dad, climbing out of the car with a big smile on his face. "Is anyone interested in helping me take out a suitcase?"

"Yes, sir," said DorJo. "I'm thinking about hiding it, too, so Arden can't go home with you."

"Oh, dear!" Mom laughed. Arden thought she sounded nervous. "You'd better wait until you've been together a while before you make statements like that!"

For a moment Arden let herself imagine what it would be

like to stand her ground, come Sunday, and absolutely refuse to return to Grierson. Maybe she could do it. Maybe, by Sunday, it would be all set.

"Mama's gone grocery shopping, but she said for y'all to come on in," DorJo said.

Dad glanced at his watch. "Well, much as we'd like to, I'm afraid we'll have to leave right away to claim our motel reservation by six. We'll visit on Sunday afternoon when we come back through—around three."

DorJo quickly unloaded the suitcase and set it on the porch. Arden told Dad and Mom goodbye. They watched the car drive up the street toward the highway; then, moved by the same impulse, they let out a whoop and hugged each other once more.

"Come on," said DorJo. "You got to see my room. Mama bought me new curtains and a bedspread."

Between them, they lugged the heavy suitcase into the house. DorJo went first, to open the screen door. Once inside, Arden stopped and looked around. The house seemed smaller than she remembered, but the smell was the same. She smiled. Another piece slipped into place.

"Hurry up!" DorJo called from the bedroom. "What're you doing out there?"

"Just smelling things," Arden said, heading toward DorJo's room just beside the kitchen. "I'm coming."

DorJo took Arden's arm and pulled her into the room. "Look!"

Frilly curtains with pink and white checks and a bedspread to match brightened the small space like a happy smile. DorJo and pink ruffles! To think that only a little over a year ago she had been the terror of the sixth grade, boys included. Back then, she would never have dreamed of frills, or if she had, no one would ever have known about it.

154

"It's just beautiful, Dor!" Arden said. "It's the prettiest room I ever saw." In her mind, she saw the blue room in Grierson, huge and formal even with her stuff scattered about. She did not want to go back to it.

The picture of herself that she had given DorJo on moving day was still stuck in the frame of the bureau mirror, its edges curled slightly inward. Another picture in a frame sat just beneath it, a boy whom Arden didn't recognize.

"Who is that?" she asked, moving closer to look.

"Bobby Hedgepeth. He just moved here a couple of weeks after you left. He's in the eighth grade."

"Are you . . . is he . . . your boyfriend?"

DorJo laughed unselfconsciously. "No—at least he don't know about it. A whole bunch of us were trading school pictures. He has one of me, too—me and about a dozen other girls."

"What does your mama say?" Arden asked, remembering Mrs. Huggins's hostility toward boys.

"Nothing." DorJo snorted. "She don't mind pictures, as long as the real person don't start hanging around." She heaved Arden's suitcase onto the bed. "Gosh, you must have bricks in here! What did you bring that weighs so much?"

"You sound like Dad. It's just clothes. I didn't know what to bring, so I put in everything." She hesitated, then said, "He said it felt as if I put enough clothes in to stay for good."

"I wish you *could* stay for good," DorJo said, plopping herself on the chair by the bed.

Arden's heart warmed. After the experience with Nina and Judy, it was good to know that she had, indeed, been missed. "I wish it, too," she said. "In fact—"

She stopped, suddenly cautious. Did she dare tell DorJo?

"In fact what?" DorJo prompted.

"In fact, I wish it a lot lately," Arden said, backing away

from telling what she had in mind. "I wish it every day, and lately, two or three times a day. Grierson is not the place for me. I don't belong there. It hasn't gotten any better. I think it's worse."

"You look different," DorJo commented, cocking her head to one side. "I've been trying to figure out what it is."

Arden turned quickly and looked into the mirror. Same pigtails, sweatshirt, face. She shrugged. "I'm thinner, maybe, because of the flu."

"Oh, well!" DorJo dismissed the subject with a leap from the chair. "Open the suitcase and let's get your stuff put away before Mama gets here. We'll help her start supper, then we can go out. Where do you want to go first?"

"Everywhere!" Arden said, as she undid the clasps on the suitcase. "Everywhere at once!"

CHAPTER SIXTEEN

"SETH SAID TO GO OVER AS SOON AS YOU GOT HERE," DORJO
explained, as they hurried along the road to Seth's house just
outside of town. "Even if it was late afternoon."

"How *is* Seth?" asked Arden. "I wrote to him, but he never
answered."

"Okay. I never see him except at school."

"You mean you haven't been rafting on the pond since I
left?"

"Naw. The weather's been too cold. Besides, it might look
funny, just him and me."

That seemed a peculiar remark coming from DorJo, who
had never cared what anyone thought. Arden studied her friend
as they walked along. She still had the short, neat haircut that
Jessie had given her last summer. Arden noticed that she had
had her ears pierced. Tiny silver hearts on each lobe gave her
a grownup look. Instead of the faded, stretched T-shirt she
used to wear, she now had on a lilac cotton blouse with tiny
flowers embroidered at the neck.

"Does he ever talk about his heart?" Arden asked.

To her surprise, DorJo laughed. "Well, not in the way you mean," she said. "But he *has* got him a girlfriend."

Arden could not account for the strange feeling that came over her then. "Oh," she said. "Is it anyone I know?"

"Patsy Johnson."

Arden thought about Seth and Patsy Johnson. Back in the sixth grade, during that awful time when DorJo disappeared, Seth had been a nobody in their class. Small and pale, always on the fringes, no one paid much attention to him. In those times, Patsy Johnson wouldn't give him the time of day.

"She's bigger than he is," Arden said.

"Not anymore," replied DorJo.

It was nearly five by the time they reached Seth's house. The pond behind it looked the same, its bluish-green surface barely rippling in the mild breeze. The stand of trees on the far side seemed to grow out of the water itself. The short pier maintained its sturdy vigil, but there was no sign of the raft. Instead, a rowboat drifted at the end of a mooring rope tied to the pier. In it sat Seth and Patsy Johnson.

Seth had caught sight of them and was waving and calling to them to come down to the boat. They crossed the new green grass and walked down the slight incline to the water's edge. As they approached, Arden experienced a shock. How could Seth change that much in three months? He was definitely larger, his hair was darker, and his voice had become husky. Blond Patsy in white pants and a blue top smiled and waved, too, but it was clear that Seth was the person she was mainly interested in.

"Well, here she is," DorJo announced, pointing at Arden. "I told you we'd come."

Seth was glad to see her—Arden could tell that much—

158

but there was something reserved about him, too. He didn't get out of the boat. Arden wondered if he was afraid he'd have to hug her.

"We didn't know if you'd ever come back," he said, grinning.

"I had doubts about it myself," she said, sitting on the grass right at the water's edge. "It wasn't because I didn't want to."

"It seems like you've hardly been gone," Patsy said.

Arden was silent. Maybe the person who left always noticed the departure more than the ones who stayed.

"It don't seem like that to me," DorJo said loyally. "It feels like she's been gone a year."

"You look different," said Seth.

"So do you," she said.

There was an awkward pause, then Seth said, "Y'all want to ride in the boat?" Patsy slid over to make room for another person on the stern seat.

"Where's the raft?" Arden asked, looking around.

"It rotted. I chopped it up for firewood."

She felt a little spasm of sadness. A rowboat wasn't the same as the raft. You couldn't lie down on it and look up at the trees and sky. You had to sit in one place and not move around suddenly.

"Come on," said Seth. "One of you sit beside Patsy. The other can sit in the bow."

After some maneuvering, they were all settled in the boat. Arden shared the stern seat with Patsy. Their shoulders touched as they faced Seth sitting in the middle seat with oars ready. DorJo, in the bow, untied the rope, and Seth leaned forward on the oars, moving the boat away from the pier. Arden could see the muscles in his upper arms straining. It occurred to her that maybe with his damaged heart he shouldn't be doing this. She wondered if Patsy knew about his heart.

"Me and Patsy are going over to my uncle's skating rink in Porterfield tonight," he said. "Y'all want to go?"

Arden was close enough to Patsy to hear the other girl's sharp intake of breath, and to see her hands, which had been resting on her knees, clasp each other tightly. It was plain that Seth had not consulted her before issuing the invitation.

Looking over Seth's head, Arden caught DorJo's eye. "I don't think we can," she said. "We've got plans."

"Yeah," said DorJo. "Thanks anyway."

Patsy's hands relaxed. Arden wondered if Seth even noticed. They rowed around the pond. Was it her imagination, or was the pond smaller than she remembered? She thought of goldfish swimming around and around in a bowl. The sun dipped lower, brushing the treetops, casting long shadows across the water. She wanted to be somewhere else.

"We have to go," DorJo said. "Mama's prob'ly got supper ready."

"Well, you hardly just got here," Seth said, but he rowed back to the pier to let them out. He waved goodbye, with some vague words about seeing her again maybe before she left.

Arden and DorJo walked up the hill to the road. When they were out of earshot, Arden said, "Having Patsy there sort of messed things up, didn't it?"

"Yeah . . . that's the thing about this girlfriend stuff. She's jealous."

"Of us? But *we* weren't ever Seth's girlfriends!"

"I know, but we are his friends and we are girls, and I guess people like Patsy can't draw but one conclusion from that."

"That's dumb!" Arden griped, scuffing her toes in the grass along the roadside. "It takes away all the fun."

160

"I guess so," DorJo said, but she didn't sound too upset about it.

Arden awoke in the middle of the night not knowing where she was. A faint light came in through the window, but the window wasn't in the right place. She lay puzzling for a few seconds, then, turning over, she remembered she was back in Haverlee and DorJo was sleeping soundly in the bed beside her. She smiled in the dark. What a happy moment, to wake up exactly where she wanted to be!

She turned over again, restless and wide awake. The silence around her was different from the sounds of Grierson, where all through the night one heard sirens, revving truck engines, trains, loud music. Even in a quiet neighborhood those noises filtered in, until finally a person just accepted them as background. She had forgotten how quiet it could be here. It was so still she felt that she could almost hear an ant tiptoe across the floor.

Precious time was slipping away. Even as she lay here, the hour of her departure drew closer. Sometime tomorrow afternoon, her visit would be half over. From then on, the minutes would gather speed like the downward ride of a roller coaster, and, before she knew it, she would be in the car on the way back to Grierson.

Maybe.

They were out of the house by eight-thirty next morning, leaving Mrs. Huggins to sleep late. The day was bright and dewy, the air full of the smell of new growth. It was not lost on Arden that the weather was perfect, just more evidence of the magic of this place.

"I want to visit the hideout and go see Granpa Huggins," she said. "And I want to go by the school, just to look at it.

Maybe we can walk up and down the streets so I can see people." She fingered the key in her pocket but did not mention it to DorJo. That would be a surprise for later.

"Well, since everybody's still in bed this early in the morning, why don't we go to the hideout first?" DorJo suggested.

"Good," said Arden. "This early in the day no one will see us." She and DorJo had always made a big deal of approaching the hideout by a complicated and indirect route, just in case someone followed them.

DorJo gave her a funny look. "That don't matter anymore, Arden," she said, the way a grownup speaks to a child.

"No, I guess not," Arden mumbled.

When they were almost at the clay bluffs where the cave hideout was, Arden asked, "Have you been here lately?"

"Not since you and I were here together last summer," DorJo said. "I . . . seems like I didn't want to come by myself."

The cave was actually a hole that had eroded beneath the roots of trees growing at the edge of the bluffs. During the years that it had been their hideout, they had camouflaged it with the honeysuckle and kudzu that grew in abundance all around. That way a person standing only a few feet away couldn't see the opening. Today, though, as soon as they came within sight of the bluffs, they could see that someone had pulled away the protective cover and left it exposed.

Arden was first to spot the change. "Dor—look! Some nerd's been snooping around!"

DorJo stopped in her tracks and grabbed Arden's arm. "Wait a minute. Don't go rushing up. Somebody might be there right now, no telling who."

Arden was too angry to be scared. "Just wait till I find a stick! What do they think they're—"

"*Wait* a minute!" DorJo spoke more firmly this time. "Be reasonable, Arden. It don't belong to us, after all. This is a

162

free country. Maybe it's some other little kid's place now."

"Well, the least they could do would be to keep it hidden," Arden said indignantly.

"Let's go look," DorJo said.

They approached cautiously, stopping to listen at every few steps. All they could hear were the birds chirping and the whispers of wind in the tops of the tallest trees.

Right away they saw that the intruders had not been little kids. Several beer cans lay around the foot of the bluff, along with scraps of paper and plastic bags that looked as though they'd been there for a while.

"Bums," DorJo mumbled, surveying the litter.

Arden grabbed one of the exposed tree roots protruding from the clay. Hoisting herself up, she looked inside the cave. There she saw the sodden ashes of a fire and more beer cans. The pine straw that used to line the floor was all gone. The bits of colored glass they had used to decorate the inside had disappeared. The only remnant of their play place was one yellow plastic cup that had been split and flattened.

She let herself down, not looking at DorJo. Tears of rage stung her eyes, but she blinked them away. "I hate it!" she said. "The least they could do would be to throw away their trash."

DorJo didn't reply. She picked up one of the larger plastic bags and began filling it with cans and papers. For several minutes they worked without speaking, gathering every scrap they could find.

"I want to cover it over again," Arden said. "Maybe whoever did this was just passing through and won't be back. If we hide it with vines, maybe it'll stay clean until some . . . some kid finds it, like you did."

"Okay," said DorJo. "You start on that side and I'll start on this one. We'll pull the vines down from the top."

It took a while to loosen the vines and pull them over the opening. The sun rose higher, and with its warmth came insects that flew around the sweating girls' faces. Their hands and arms were scratched and prickling. Arden stood back and surveyed the work, wiping her forehead with the back of one hand.

"I believe it's almost as good as it used to be," she said. "Don't you think so?"

DorJo nodded, breathing a sigh. "I sure never expected to spend Saturday morning doing this, though."

Arden looked at the Timex. Almost ten o'clock! "Oh, Dor— I'm sorry. I . . . guess I got carried away."

"It's okay," said DorJo. "Come on, let's go back."

They walked without talking. Arden's hands, dry with dirt, itched. With a pang, she realized that she never wanted to see the hideout again.

CHAPTER SEVENTEEN

THE SUN WAS DIRECTLY OVERHEAD WHEN THE TWO OF THEM, followed by the lean dogs of Hardy Street, trudged back home after a visit with Granpa Huggins. Arden had been alarmed at how the old man had wasted away. He seemed to have gotten smaller and he coughed a great deal. He joked with them, told Arden he missed seeing her around town, and gave them each a bar of the chocolate candy he always seemed to have on hand. But none of that hid the weariness in his eyes.

"Do Granpa and your mama get along okay now?" Arden asked, as they came to the end of Hardy Street and turned at the corner into Monday Lane. The sniffing dogs that she had once feared so much stopped at the end of the street and wagged their tails as if to say goodbye.

"Pretty much," said DorJo. "She complains sometimes about having to be responsible for him, but she does it, and that's what counts."

"And what about Jessie?"

"She don't stay with us when she comes home from Porterfield. She goes to Granpa's." DorJo sighed. "She says he needs her worse'n we do, which is the truth, but that ain't the real reason. She and Mama just can't stay in the same place for long without one or the other starting a argument."

"I'm sorry," Arden said. "Last year . . . well, it seemed as if things were going to be better."

"Things *are* better. At least they each don't try to keep me away from the other, like last year. And everybody's close by. That's better, ain't it?"

Arden had to agree. After all, she had once been frightened of Mrs. Huggins, but now she knew that the woman was more bluster than bite. Arden made up her mind to do everything she could to please DorJo's mother during this visit. That way, when she asked the Big Question, the answer was more likely to be yes.

Mrs. Huggins, looking more rested than the night before, had fixed sandwiches and iced tea for their lunch. "I figured you'd be traipsing all over town," she said, "and you'd be wore out and hungry."

"Thanks, Mama," DorJo said. "We'll make supper tonight."

"It'll be fun to do some cooking," Arden said to Mrs. Huggins. "I don't get a chance now that Gran's in charge."

"How're you getting along in Grierson anyhow?" Mrs. Huggins asked, as they sat down to eat.

"All right, I guess." Arden looked at her plate.

"You don't like it much, do you?"

"No, ma'am."

"Well," said Mrs. Huggins, cutting her sandwich in two, "don't fight against it too hard. You're there, you need to make the best of it."

"I wish I could come back here," Arden murmured, but

Mrs. Huggins didn't appear to hear. She turned to DorJo and asked, "How's your granpa?"

"Pretty good." DorJo was noncommittal. She took a bite of sandwich and appeared to be done with the subject of Granpa.

"I didn't think he looked so good," Arden spoke up.

DorJo stopped chewing. She sent Arden a kind of warning look.

"Oh?" said Mrs. Huggins. The word put Arden on guard. "How do you mean?"

Arden stumbled a bit, backpedaling. "He's a little thinner, is all. He's in great spirits, though. Jokes just like always— said he missed me. I don't know if he did or not, but it made me feel good." She hated the gushy way she sounded, like a Grierson town girl or something. What had she gotten into?

"That old man is on his last legs," Mrs. Huggins said. "He knows it, I know it. It ain't going to be long before he has to go in a hospital, and I don't know what in the world we'll do for money to pay the doctor bills." Her left hand worried the paper napkin beside her plate. Her tone was both angry and sad.

"Aw, he's all right, Mama," DorJo said. "Arden just ain't seen him in a long time. He's not worse."

"You don't fool me," Mrs. Huggins said. "I was over there last week. I can see for myself."

Arden ate steadily, wondering how to change the subject. Granpa couldn't help being sick; it seemed unfair to be mad at him for it.

"This is a good sandwich," she said.

"Thanks—I'm glad you like it. DorJo, was he coughing?" Mrs. Huggins said it all without missing a beat.

"No more than usual."

"I guess I'll have to take off work next week and get him to

167

a doctor. I swear, there's no end to it. I don't get paid when I don't work, but he won't get to no doctor if I don't take him."

Her voice rose as she talked, spinning a web of anxiety around them.

"Don't worry about it," DorJo said. "Granpa's okay."

"That's easy for you to say!" Mrs. Huggins snapped. "A person can't just close their eyes to what's coming. Somebody's got to plan ahead."

Why didn't I keep my mouth shut? thought Arden. The sandwich was thick and dry. She sat straight, her back stiff with the tension at the table. If talking about Granpa was off limits, DorJo should have told her. The more out of sorts Mrs. Huggins became, the more difficult it would be for her to listen to Arden later.

"We'll clean up the lunch stuff," DorJo said gruffly when Mrs. Huggins finally wound down. "Then we're going out again. We'll be back by four to start supper."

"Suit yourself," Mrs. Huggins said shortly. "I might take a nap, myself."

"I'm sorry for what I said about Granpa," Arden said when they left the house later. "I was just making conversation. I didn't realize it would cause trouble."

"That's all right." DorJo didn't seem to want to talk about it.

"I don't understand why she got so upset," Arden went on.

"Because she's scared," said DorJo. "When you said he looked worse, that just made her think about how close the time is when he can't take care of himself anymore."

"Oh," said Arden, sort of understanding. Still, it was very different from the way her own family would handle such a problem. She wouldn't mention Granpa around Mrs. Huggins again.

168

Haverlee School looked lonely, as schools do on Saturdays. The doors were closed and locked, the shades in all the windows half lowered. DorJo and Arden walked all the way around the outside of both the elementary and the high-school buildings. She had never thought of it as being either large or small, but after going to Brinks for three months, Haverlee School appeared to her to have shrunk. The old part that had been built in the twenties seemed even older now.

"I sure do miss it," Arden said. "I'd do most anything to come back here." She went over and sat on one of the steps at the front of the gym.

"Why do you hate Grierson so bad?" DorJo asked, sitting beside her. "Ain't there anything good about it?"

"No," said Arden without hesitation.

"Haven't you met anybody you like—or any*thing?*"

"Well, there was Faye—I told you about her in one of my letters—but she moved away. And there's Tyrone."

"Is he your boyfriend?"

"No," said Arden. "He's just a friend. He sings in the chorus. The chorus is pretty good, but that's all. It's not enough."

"Well," said DorJo, "I'm sorry you hate it, since you live there."

"Dor—what would your mama say if I asked her to let me live with you till school's out?"

DorJo's dark eyes probed hers. "Are you serious?"

Arden nodded. "I've been thinking about it for days. I told my folks it's what I want to do. They say no. Now I'm ready to do something desperate."

"That don't sound like you, Arden."

"Well, what can a person do? It's not fair—they let Hill do what he wanted to do. Why can't they do the same for me?"

"What do they say?" DorJo asked.

"The main thing they say is that I don't have relatives here to live with, the way Hill did. But if . . . if your mama would be willing to let me live with you—I mean, if it was *really* all right and she said so—then they might change their minds. What do you think she'd say?"

She waited, scarcely breathing, for DorJo's answer.

"You'll have to ask her," said DorJo finally.

"Do you think she'd say no?"

"I don't know. But she'll tell you flat out. You have to be ready to hear her answer, whatever it is. Mama always says what she thinks, sometimes two or three times, so you'll get the point."

DorJo stood up and swiped at the backside of her jeans to brush off the dust. "Where do you want to go now?"

Arden got up slowly, fingering the key in the bottom of her pocket. "I think . . . I'd like to go over to my house."

"Sure," said DorJo. "But won't that bother you, just standing outside looking at it?"

Arden brought forth the key and held it up. It glinted in the sunlight. "I brought this. We can go inside."

DorJo's eyes widened, but she didn't ask any questions. "Come on then. We have about an hour before we have to go home."

They jumped a ditch and crossed the street, heading back to the middle of town. If DorJo really wanted her back, wouldn't she say so? Wouldn't she act pleased at the idea? Doubt gnawed at Arden. She rubbed the key, wondering what magic would rise from it to grant her wish.

With DorJo following close behind, she went up on the porch of the empty house and inserted the key in the lock, as she had done so often before. A sharp twist to the left and the lock clicked. "There!" She breathed. "Let's go."

"Whew! It smells in here!" exclaimed DorJo, wrinkling her

nose. Her voice echoed hollowly. "And it seems like night with the drapes closed. Couldn't we open 'em enough to see our way around?"

"Sure—why not?" Arden stepped into the room where their dining table and Mom's corner cabinet had once stood. It was bare now. She pulled the drapery cord and watched the dust motes fly up in the light that suddenly flooded the room. "Let's open all the windows," she said. "The air has been trapped in here since December. No wonder it smells!"

"Are you sure it's okay?"

"Of course! Yesterday Dad was talking about coming in to make the house feel better . . . but we didn't have time." She didn't add that he didn't know she had the key and that she hadn't told him. "You take the downstairs, I'll take the upstairs."

Arden entered the room that had been hers. Now the only thing familiar about it was the window seat. She crossed to it and peered out the window. Down below she saw the backyard, with its large trees putting out new green buds. Mom's azaleas were blooming, too, and the dogwood at the corner of the fence.

DorJo came and stood in the doorway. "Seeing you in this room makes me feel like I'm looking at a ghost,"she said.

Arden smiled, remembering the time when she and DorJo had shared this room like sisters. As she turned back to look out once more, the plan came to her suddenly, like a gift. It almost took her breath away, it was so perfect.

"Dor! How would you like to live in this house?"

Without even looking, she felt DorJo's astonishment. "What're you talking about, Arden?"

"Well, no one's shown any interest in buying or renting it. And Dad said yesterday he wished someone was living in it, even if they were only renting. So I was thinking—if your mama and you would move over here and pay Dad just the same amount of rent you pay for the house on Purdue Street, it would help Dad and it would give you more room. If Granpa has to come stay with you, there'd be plenty of room for him." And, she added to herself, for me, too.

DorJo didn't answer right away. The gleam of interest in her eyes was followed quickly by reservation. "Move over," she said.

Arden made room for her on the window seat. "Don't you think it's a good idea?"

"I don't know." DorJo's answer was guarded. "You know how Mama is. I don't think she'd like it that she wasn't paying the amount of rent the house is worth. She'd say she was taking charity. And she can't pay more than she already is."

"But don't you see—right now Dad's not getting anything. Whatever she paid would be better than *that*. She'd be doing us a favor."

"Does he know about this idea?" DorJo asked.

"No, but he'll like it. I'm sure he will."

"I don't know. What if your Dad don't want to rent to us? Or what if he does, but Mama don't want to move? There's too many people have to be convinced for me to get in a uproar."

Arden got up and moved restlessly around the empty room, listening to the echo. "I guess the first step is to find out how Dad feels about it," she said, "so we'll have to wait until tomorrow afternoon before we mention it to your mama. I wish—"

She stopped suddenly and listened. "Dor—did you hear something downstairs?"

"We left the front door unlocked. Maybe somebody wandered in off the street," DorJo whispered, coming to stand beside her. Voices floated up from the hallway below. "What do we do now?"

"Go down and tell whoever it is to get out," Arden said, licking dry lips. "In a nice way, of course."

They went out into the hall, Arden in the lead. At the foot of the stairs gazing up at them were two women and a man. "*Might* I ask what you two girls are doing here?" asked one of the women. She had dark brown curly hair and long, sharp fingernails.

"I'm Arden Gifford. This house belongs to my mom and dad." She hoped she sounded cool and a shade indignant. "I was going to ask you the same question."

"Oh," said the woman in a somewhat friendlier tone. "I'm Sheila Barrow from Nottingham Realty. This is Mr. and Mrs. Ludlow—they came to see the house. Your name is . . . Arden, did you say?"

"Yes. This is my friend, DorJo Huggins." She wouldn't come down any farther, not wishing to shake anyone's hand. The man was short and stocky. His wife, not much taller than Arden, looked as though she was expecting a baby.

"It gave me quite a start to see all the windows open and to find the door unlocked," said Ms. Barrow. "I thought vagrants had broken in."

"I have a key," Arden said.

"Oh. Are your parents here, then?"

"No. They're at the beach. I'm visiting." She didn't think she would tell Ms. Barrow that Mom and Dad would be back tomorrow.

"I see. Well, you girls will excuse us while we look around a bit. The Ludlows are moving here from Virginia." Ms. Barrow gave the couple a bright smile, then winked at Arden. "We may have some news for your folks before the weekend is over. Would you girls mind closing the windows before you go? We want to make sure it doesn't rain in and ruin the carpet, don't we?"

Arden refused to be counted as Ms. Barrow's conspirator. "We'll close them when we leave," she said.

Ms. Barrow turned to the Ludlows. "Come along—we'll look at the backyard first," she said. "We'll go over the house when the girls are through."

She flashed a look at Arden and DorJo which seemed to say, You'd better be out of here when I get back. "Goodbye, girls."

"Well," said DorJo when they heard the door slam. "There goes that idea."

"What idea?" Arden said, still brooding.

"They'll buy the house. So your idea about Mama and me moving in won't work. I sure am glad I didn't get excited about it."

"People have looked at it before," Arden said. "Nobody's bought it. They won't either—you'll see."

"Looks like you'd be glad," DorJo said. "If it gets sold, y'all can buy your own house and then you won't have to live with your gran anymore. Come on, let's close the windows."

"She has no right to run us out," Arden said stonily. "We can stay here as long as we like."

"But I promised Mama we'd be back by four to start supper," DorJo reminded her. "We've got thirty minutes to close the windows and get home."

Defeated, Arden nodded. "Okay. Go ahead."

As she made her way around each room, closing windows, she felt numb. What sort of justice would let such a wonderful plan come to her full-blown, only to have it snatched away by Ms. Barrow of Nottingham Realty?

174

All the way back to DorJo's house, Arden nursed disappointment.

"Don't let it get you down," DorJo said. "I don't think
it would've worked. There was too much to go wrong
anyhow."

"I'm okay," Arden lied. "It might work out, still. Those
people may not buy the house." But she found it hard to
believe her own words.

CHAPTER EIGHTEEN

"ARDEN'S GOT SOMETHING TO ASK YOU, MAMA," DORJO SAID, after the dishes were washed and Mrs. Huggins had just turned on the TV. Arden thought the timing was bad—Mrs. Huggins wanted to watch the program—but time was terribly short. Tomorrow morning, Mrs. Huggins would leave the house before the girls got up. She wouldn't be back until just before Arden would have to leave. Things had to be settled one way or the other before that.

"What is it?" Mrs. Huggins's impatient gaze turned in Arden's direction.

Although she had rehearsed the words a hundred times, Arden suddenly forgot everything she intended to say. All she could think of was The Question.

"What would you think if I came here to live?" she asked in a rush. "If I paid for my food and my part of the rent and all? It would just be until the end of the school year. I'd go back to Grierson in the summer."

She kept her eyes on Mrs. Huggins while she spoke, watch-

176

ing for signs of change, but Mrs. Huggins's gaze was steady and listening.

"I thought you girls prob'ly had that up your sleeve," she said after a moment.

"DorJo didn't," Arden said. "It was my idea."

Mrs. Huggins reached over and turned down the sound. "We could use the extra money," she said.

"Mama!" DorJo said, shocked.

"Well, we could," Mrs. Huggins said. "No need to pretend about it. But I don't think it's a very good idea."

"Why not?" DorJo asked. Arden was thankful that her friend asked the question for her.

But instead of answering DorJo, Mrs. Huggins turned back to Arden. "Tell me why you want to come here instead of staying with your family."

"Grierson's an awful place," she said. "People there are so phony! The school is huge—a person feels lost, and nobody cares whether you live or die. I want to come back here to Haverlee where people know each other and care about each other—"

Mrs. Huggins interrupted with a little snort of derision. "Honey, let me tell you it isn't all roses in a little town like this! The way folks tend to each other's business is a pain in the ass. At least living in the city you don't have the neighbors breathing down your neck tellin' you what they think you ought to do!"

Arden didn't know how to reply. "I'd just like it better here," she said lamely.

"What do your folks say?"

"They're against it." She looked at a spot on the floor near Mrs. Huggins's sandaled feet.

"They say why?"

Arden nodded. "They think I have more 'advantages' in

177

Grierson." She stretched the word mockingly. "I'm not interested in advantages."

"What else?"

"They said you might not have room for me," she said. "But mostly they say it imposes on people who aren't family." She waited for Mrs. Huggins to deny that it was so.

Mrs. Huggins crossed one knee over the other and swung her foot back and forth. She looked vacantly at the soundless picture on the TV screen and chewed on the side of one fingernail. DorJo and Arden exchanged looks, but they knew better than to say anything.

"Let me tell you something, Arden." Mrs. Huggins said, turning suddenly to look her in the eye. "For a girl your age, the best thing is to be with your own family, even if you don't like where they live."

"But I'm so miserable!"

"Why do you think I came back here and took charge of my house again?" Mrs. Huggins asked bluntly. It was the first time she had ever alluded to her past around Arden. "I'll tell you why. I didn't want somebody else raisin' my young'un, that's why. I missed out with Jessie, I know that, but I'm not about to make that mistake again. Your folks feel the same. They don't want somebody else raisin' you."

"But you wouldn't be raising me—"

"Well, I would, too! While you were here, you'd sure have to do things my way."

Arden was taken aback. She hadn't thought of that before.

"Besides that, we ain't got a lot of the things you're used to," Mrs. Huggins said. "You and DorJo'd have to squeeze up in that little room together."

"I wouldn't mind, Mama," DorJo said in a low voice.

"Maybe not," said Mrs. Huggins, "at least not for the first few days. But then you'd start gettin' on each other's nerves."

178

Mrs. Huggins said the same things Mom and Dad did. How in the world could a person ever win an argument with a grownup? They always thought they knew ahead of time how a thing would turn out.

"Mrs. Huggins," Arden began, licking dry lips. She knew she shouldn't say it but desperation made her. "What if . . . my Dad would be willing for you to rent our house for the same amount as you're renting this one? Would you move over there? There'd be lots of room."

Mrs. Huggins stared at her as though she had taken leave of her senses. "Now, whose idea was *that?*"

"Mine," she admitted.

"I thought so." Mrs. Huggins shook her head. "Arden, do you have any idea the difference of my rent and the rent of a house like that?"

"But they're not getting *any*thing for it now. The rent you paid would be something—"

"It wouldn't even pay the taxes. Us livin' there would just get in the way of selling the house. Your daddy wouldn't think of it. You can just put it out of your mind."

Arden felt like crying, or perhaps more like whimpering, the way she used to do when she was little and had an earache.

"I know it's hard," Mrs. Huggins said with unexpected understanding. "I wouldn't mind lettin' DorJo come to visit you when summer gets here."

Arden nodded. Mrs. Huggins leaned forward and turned up the sound.

"Come on," DorJo said. She got up from her chair and signaled for Arden to follow her outside.

They sat side by side on the porch in the dark, elbows on knees, looking up at the clear night sky. Tears dripped down Arden's face. After a while, DorJo spoke in a low voice.

"I wish she'd said yes."

"Yeah—me too."

"When Mama thinks something, it's hard to change her mind."

"I didn't know she was so hot on family," Arden said.

"Well, what happened last year made her see things different," said DorJo. "Now that she's got her family together more or less, she thinks everybody else ought to do the same."

Arden sighed. "Yesterday, I was about ninety-nine percent sure I wasn't going back, even if I had to camp over at the house in secret."

"It ain't like your family is awful to live with," DorJo said. "If they beat up on you, Mama would let you stay here, no question about it. But she knows how nice your family is. Just think, what if they were awful *and* you had to live in Grierson, too? At least your situation is *partly* all right."

Arden was not comforted. The days of her life seemed to stretch out before her, full of testing and monotony.

At two o'clock on Sunday afternoon, DorJo and Arden sat on the porch again, this time waiting for Dad and Mom to return from the beach. The sky had begun to cloud over, giving the day a flatness that matched Arden's mood.

They had run out of things to do and talk about. It was the first time that had happened in all the time they'd known each other.

"Is there someplace you'd like to go?" DorJo asked. "Maybe over to your house to see if those folks bought it?"

"No." Arden shook her head. "I don't want to know."

DorJo sighed a little. "I'm afraid you didn't have a very good time this weekend. I'm real sorry."

"Hey, wait a minute!" Arden protested. "I did *so* have a good time!"

"Then why are we sitting here like two bumps on a log?"

Three or four answers crowded to Arden's lips at once, but none of them seemed worthy of DorJo's honest question.

"Well, anyway, it's not your fault," she said finally.

DorJo's eyes were full of sympathy. She looked as though she wanted to say something but wasn't sure she should.

"What is it?" Arden asked.

"It'll sound like I'm preaching," DorJo warned.

Arden managed a smile. "Well, if I'm going to be preached at, I'd rather it be you than somebody else."

"I was just going to say that since you've got to go back to Grierson anyway, maybe you could start trying to see the good of it."

Arden didn't want to hear it, but she kept her mouth shut so that DorJo could finish.

"You don't have to love it like you loved Haverlee," DorJo went on. "But you don't have to hate it, either. There's bound to be something there to make it bearable."

Give up hating Grierson? How could she stop, just like that?

"Well, think about it," DorJo finished. "I guess all I need to say is that where you live don't keep me from being your friend. Maybe everything else has changed, but not that."

Arden, looking at her friend, felt a lump settle in her throat. "Yeah," she said. "Me, too."

Dad and Mom arrived shortly before three. Their faces were pink. They looked relaxed and smiley. Dad leaped from the car. "Well, how did you two get along?" he wanted to know. "Did you have a good time?"

"It was great!" Arden said. "We've been everywhere, seen everybody. We've hardly had an extra minute!" She didn't look at DorJo while she raved. DorJo would understand why she was doing this.

"Uh-oh," Dad said. "Does that mean we have to kidnap you to get you to go back with us?"

181

She knew by the way he asked the question that he was expecting her to plant her feet in the black dirt and say, "I'm not going home!" Maybe they'd already decided they would give in and let her have her way after all.

"No," she said, turning away. "Of course not. I'll get my suitcase."

"Mama will be disappointed if y'all don't stay and visit a little bit this time," DorJo said. "She'll be back from work just any minute now."

"I'd love to," Mom said, getting out of the car. "I've been cramped into this front seat forever. I need to stretch my legs."

Arden noticed that Mom's arms were pink, too, the color of lightly boiled shrimp. She wore blue slacks and a matching top, and she looked just the way she used to before they moved to Grierson, full of energy and good humor.

"You must have had a good time, too," she said to them.

"Best thing that ever happened," Dad said, winking at Mom. "I shed ten years."

Ten years. Arden thought about it. If she had shed ten years she'd be three years old. It seemed to her that she had added ten years, if anything. She felt heavy and tired.

Soon Mrs. Huggins returned from work. Her blue uniform was wrinkled and she was clearly tired, but she was glad to see the Giffords.

"It's been nice having Arden here," she said as she shook Dad's hand and hugged Mom in greeting. "She and DorJo took up right where they left off at."

"Good!" said Dad. "Sometimes a long-distance move can kill a friendship."

"Well, not this one." Mrs. Huggins settled herself in a chair, taking the lemonade DorJo offered. "Now, tell me all about yourself."

182

Arden and DorJo sat quietly side by side on the sofa, listening to the grownups talk about jobs and the cost of buying a car. After a while, Dad looked at his watch and announced that they must leave if they were going to get back to Grierson before dark. "We stayed away as long as we could," he said to Mrs. Huggins, "so that Mother could enjoy having the house to herself for two whole days."

"I expect that does feel good to her," Mrs. Huggins said. "A bunch of people can crowd up a house quicker'n you realize."

Oh gee, here it comes, Arden thought, expecting Mrs. Huggins to say something about her asking to move in with them, but she only said, "Anytime Arden wants to come back this way, you let her, you hear?"

"Well, take one last look, Bird," Dad said, as he drove the car along the street headed back toward the highway.

"I don't need to," Arden said flatly. "I've been looking at it for two days."

"It's a nice little town," Mom mused. "Too bad we had to leave so suddenly."

Arden had never felt so empty. Empty of hopefulness. The trip to Haverlee had hung before her like a bright star for these past few weeks. Now she had nothing to look forward to, and she knew that this magic kingdom was gone for good.

As they approached the edge of town, she suddenly remembered the key in her pocket, and then she thought of Ms. Barrow.

"I meant to tell you," she said, leaning forward. "The lady from Nottingham showed the house to some people from Virginia yesterday. She said she might have some news for you."

Dad put his foot on the brake. "Sure enough? Did you tell her we'd be here this afternoon?"

"Well . . . no."

Dad pulled the car over to the side of the street. Then he turned and gave her a searching look. "Why didn't you?"

"Yes," Mom said. "You should have told us as soon as we got to DorJo's."

"I forgot," said Arden. It was true, she had forgotten. She reached into her pocket and pulled out the key. "Here—I brought it from Grierson, so I could get into the house. DorJo and I were there yesterday when Ms. Barrow brought the people. The lady's going to have a baby."

She laid the key in Dad's outstretched palm and sat back, folding her arms. She waited for the questions which were sure to follow.

Dad handed the key to Mom, who put it in her purse. "Well," he said. "Well."

"Perhaps we'd better go to Delway's Grocery and call Ms. Barrow before we leave town," Mom suggested. "It would be a shame to go all the way back to Grierson and then discover there was something we needed to do while we were here."

"Good idea," said Dad. "*If* she's in the office. Sunday afternoons are prime time for showing houses." He drove the few yards up the street to Delway's parking lot.

"Here's a quarter," said Mom, handing him the coin. "Call Ms. Barrow collect."

"If she sells the house she can deduct it," Dad said with a grin. "We'll make her itemize."

Arden watched as he disappeared into the store. She knew a few of the people who were standing around outside, but unlike on Friday, she didn't want to speak to anyone now. She was tired, almost as tired as when she was getting over the flu. She wondered why Mom didn't ask about the key. She would tell, if asked. She might even tell the plan that

184

would have enabled her to stay in Haverlee, if anyone asked. But Mom didn't say a word.

The minutes ticked by. Arden lay down on the back seat and closed her eyes.

When she awakened, the car was moving and Mom and Dad were deep in conversation. She opened her eyes and listened.

"I can hardly believe it, after all these months," Mom said. "In fact, I'm afraid to *let* myself believe it. I want so much for us to have our own house."

"Yes, I do, too. You and Arden were right, you know, about our living with Mother. We shouldn't have done it. Sometimes I think it would have been better for everyone if I had gone on to Grierson and left you and Arden here. I could have come home on weekends until we sold the house."

"I wouldn't have liked being away from you," Mom said, moving closer to him. She leaned her head on his shoulder. "Except for Arden's unhappiness, things have worked out pretty well."

Arden closed her eyes quickly, so they wouldn't know she was awake and listening. There was a brief pause in the conversation. She felt sure Mom was checking to be sure she was still asleep.

"Do you really think she had a good time?" Dad asked.

"I'm not sure." Mom sounded thoughtful. "The light has gone out of her eyes. Poor baby!"

Rage and self-pity rose up in Arden. She wanted to be petted and comforted, and she wanted to stand and lash out at anyone who tried to make a baby of her. She did not know which side to be on. She lay with her eyes closed and felt the movement of the car as it transported her back to nowhere.

CHAPTER NINETEEN

THEY ARRIVED IN GRIERSON AFTER SUNDOWN. ARDEN HAD SLEPT—
or pretended to—most of the way.

Dad looked back at Arden. "Home again, Bird," he said
cautiously. She tried to smile at him, but she could tell by
the way her face felt that it came out wrong.

She opened the rear door and climbed out, feeling wrinkled
and used up. The chilly air, hanging halfway between winter
and spring, made her shiver.

Suddenly the front door opened and Gran appeared, smiling
and waving. Arden stared. It was like a scene from the old
days, except that then Big Dad had been there, too. For a
long moment, Arden had the eerie feeling that she had been
thrown backward in time. But perhaps she was seeing the future
instead.

"Are you all right, Arden?" Mom asked, putting an arm
around her.

"Yes," she answered, not at all sure she was saying the truth.

186

Something was dawning, but she couldn't quite touch it. Something . . . about Gran.

"You're just in time!" Gran called from the porch. "I took two loaves of bread from the oven not five minutes ago!"

"What a wonderful thing to come home to," Mom said fervently. She took a deep breath. "I smell it all the way out here."

Arden followed the grownups inside. The aura of bread was almost real enough to touch. The house was spotlessly clean, the way it used to be whenever they came to visit. But if Mom and Dad noticed, they gave no indication. Perhaps they were already thinking of themselves in another house anyway. While they ate large slices of hot buttered bread, they chattered about the weekend like two kids, not leaving out the part about the possible sale of the Haverlee house. Gran merely smiled as she listened. Arden studied her. What was it?

Finally Gran turned to her. Arden waited for what would follow. *How was your weekend? Did it turn out the way you expected? How are things in Haverlee? Why did you come back?*

"I'm glad you came back," Gran said. "I wasn't sure you would. When I was baking the bread, I hoped you'd be one of the people who would be here to eat it."

Was she supposed to say thank you? The occasion seemed to call for it, but somehow Arden couldn't.

"Arden and DorJo tried to do everything in less than forty-eight hours," Mom said, smoothing over the little silence that followed Gran's words. "I think she probably needs to go to bed pretty soon to recover."

"I slept most of the way home," said Arden, aware of her grumpy tone. It was alarming to be like this. It was like turning into Mr. Hyde without intending to.

Again, a little pause. She got the feeling that the grownups were agreeing among themselves not to challenge her. They pitied her. Again the rage that she had felt in the car when Mom had said, "Poor baby!" stirred in her.

The telephone rang.

"Arden, would you answer that?" Dad said.

She got up without saying anything. They only wanted her out of the way so they could talk about her. She ambled into the hall where the telephone sat on the mahogany table. She let it ring one more time before she picked it up.

"Hey—Arden?" said a familiar voice.

"Tyrone!" She felt a surge of gladness. "Hi!"

"So you got back okay." She could hear his smile. "I was just checkin'."

"Sure, I got back," she said. "What did you expect?"

"Well," he said, "You talked a lot about stayin'. What'm I s'posed to think but you gon' do what you say?"

"I changed my mind," she said.

"I won't make out like I ain't glad," he said. "Specially now. Mr. Kale wants you and me to do a duet for the spring concert, end of April. He gimme the music Friday."

She forgot to breathe. A duet with Tyrone? In front of an auditorium full of people?

"You still there?" he asked.

"I . . . don't know," she said, gasping a little. "Tyrone, I can't do that!"

"What you mean you can't do that? You the best soprano we got, I don't care if you *are* just a seventh grader. You prob'ly the only one can sing loud enough to drown me out."

"It scares me to death!"

"Oh, you'll get over it." He chuckled a little. "I just thought you'd like to know before you come to school tomorrow." He paused, then added, "You are comin' to school tomorrow?"

She sighed, unable to help herself. "Yes. I guess so."

188

"Okay, then. Later."

She held on to the receiver for a few seconds after he had hung up, listening to the hum of the dial tone, stunned by the news. How was it possible to be so elated and so frightened at the same time? She thought she might throw up. Maybe Alice felt this way in Wonderland when she nibbled the mushroom and shot up to the ceiling. Carefully, she replaced the receiver and walked back to the dining room. Three pairs of eyes turned in her direction, their brows arched in question marks.

"Tyrone," she said.

"Oh," said Gran. "He called earlier to see if you'd gotten back yet."

Arden tensed, waiting for Gran to make some uncalled for remark, but it didn't come. Instead, Gran pushed back the chair and got to her feet.

"I'll wash these few dishes and then I'm going to bed with a good book," she said. "I've earned a rest."

Mom and Dad both laughed. Dad said, "Mother, I never thought I'd hear you say that in my lifetime."

"You should always be ready to be surprised," she said tartly, as she started for the kitchen. "Nothing's set in stone, you know!"

Nothing's set in stone, you know. The words echoed in Arden's mind as she climbed the stairs to her room with her suitcase. That was the whole trouble, of course—nothing was set in stone. If it were, a person could count on something being the same at least once in a while.

She heaved the heavy suitcase up on her bed and undid the clasps. The lid immediately popped up, straining against the overload of clothes. As she set about putting everything away, she noted that Gran had been in here, too, dusting, straightening, ordering. Her books were all in the bookcase, not leaning against one another like drunken sailors or lying on top of each other.

Had Gran snooped? She tried to think what she might have left lying about that she wouldn't want Gran to see. What business did Gran have in here anyway? Mom had always insisted that she be responsible for cleaning her own room.

She remembered suddenly quite clearly what her room had been like when she walked out of here with her suitcase on Friday morning. A pigpen, Mom would say.

She hadn't even made her bed, now that she thought about it. On impulse, she reached over and turned back the spread. Clean cases held the plump pillows. The sheets, too, were clean.

Does she want me to thank her? Arden thought fiercely as she slammed drawers and flung clothes about. What's she trying to do?

Then it occurred to her that perhaps Gran really *hadn't* expected her to come back. Maybe this was like cleaning up a person's room after they were dead, removing traces of them that would make you sad.

Arden thought about Tyrone's news that they were going to sing a duet. What if she had decided not to come back? Would Mr. Kale have picked some other girl to sing with Tyrone? Or would Tyrone have sung a solo? Would she ever have found out that Mr. Kale had chosen her? She wondered what the music was. She had forgotten to ask. Maybe it would be too hard for her. Maybe Mr. Kale would change his mind, once he heard her try to sing.

She climbed into the great bed, settling into the smell of clean sheets, but she wasn't sleepy.

Suddenly there was a knock on her door.

"Come in," she called out, expecting to see Mom. Instead, Gran's head peeped around the edge of the door.

"I thought you might have gone to sleep," she said, coming all the way in. She wore blue slippers and a blue housecoat. For an instant Arden thought of the Good Fairy, who must surely have gray hair and go about in soft blues.

"No," she said. "I was thinking."

Gran sat at the foot of the bed and looked at her closely. "About the visit?"

"Some." She waited. She thought she would scream if Gran asked whether it turned out the way she expected.

"I worried about you, to tell the truth," Gran said, talking to her directly as though they were equals. She reached over and patted Arden's hand, which lay outside the covers.

Arden felt sadness rising. "It was different from what I expected," she said stiffly. She dared Gran to gloat.

"Moving is hard," said Gran.

"People move all the time," Arden said. "It's not supposed to be any big deal. Nobody dies of it."

"But maybe sometimes they wish they would," Gran said.

Arden studied the lines of Gran's face, the brown eyes set deeply in their sockets. She thought she hadn't heard right. "Would what?" she asked.

"When you lose what you really love above all, and can't get it back no matter what, then there are times when you think that to be dead would be a fine thing. At least you wouldn't hurt anymore."

Gran looked squarely at Arden. "Maybe you think people don't understand how much you love Haverlee. But some do. Maybe they were afraid to say so, because they knew for a fact that they couldn't comfort you, even when they knew what you were going through."

191

It hit Arden then like a great light blasting through doors. They had been feeling the same thing, she and Gran, only somehow she knew that Gran's pain must exceed hers by millions of quantities. They'd coped in about the same way— by being crusty and hard to live with.

"This weekend I cried," Gran went on. She spoke as though it was hard for her to say these things. "All day Saturday I scrubbed and washed, vacuumed, straightened, polished, dusted—and cried. I thought I'd never get to the bottom of it, but this morning, for the first time since your granddad died, I woke up without that heavy rock that had been under my heart ever since November."

Gran made a fist and pressed it against the spot just under her breasts, where the rock had been. "I feel that I'm unstuck now. I don't feel so . . . so grim."

Why are you telling me this? Arden thought. Grownups weren't supposed to talk to kids about stuff like this. She didn't want to live in a world where grownups could come apart at the seams.

But she took in Gran's words all the same. She herself felt stuck. Big Dad, last summer, had talked about the wilderness—that No Place between where you'd been and where you might go. "I don't want to be stuck," she said in a whisper. "But I don't know how to get out. I don't have anyplace to go."

Gran took Arden's hand in both of hers. Arden felt their firm, dry coolness. "Well," she said, "what about the weekend?"

Arden felt the tears rising to her eyes, to her throat, but she no longer felt the need to hide them from Gran. She found herself telling how it was, sobbing and sniffing all the while, from the moment they had driven into town and weren't recognized by the people in front of the post office, until today

192

when she and DorJo had run out of things to do before their time was up. The words rushed and tumbled, defied an order of telling.

"I couldn't make things between DorJo and me be like they used to be," she said at last, wiping at her eyes with the back of her free hand. "She's still my friend—I know that. But it's different now. It doesn't help me *here*."

"You've been here three months now," Gran said. "Can you think of even one good thing?"

"Well, there's Tyrone and the chorus," Arden said, feeling herself become defensive again. "Mr. Kale wants us to do a duet in the spring concert."

Gran's eyes lit up. "Why, Arden—I had no idea you could sing that well!"

"Me either," she confessed. "It's been my favorite thing in school. I've learned a lot about music from Mr. Kale, but I didn't . . . don't think I'm good enough to sing a duet with Tyrone. He's *really* good."

Gran squeezed Arden's hand tightly. "That is absolutely wonderful, Arden! Your granddad would be so proud!"

"Tyrone's black," Arden said, thinking maybe Gran hadn't picked up on that when she talked to him on the phone.

Gran looked at her blankly. "Does that bother you?" she asked after a moment.

"N . . . no," said Arden. "But I figured it would bother *you*."

"Why on earth did you think that?"

Arden shrugged. "You just seemed so hot on me getting in with that crowd of girls you used to teach. I guess I figured you wouldn't approve of the people I really liked, like Faye and Tyrone."

"Well," said Gran, "I just didn't want you to feel stranded when you came here. I suppose I didn't give you enough credit for finding your own friends."

She let go of Arden's hand then and folded her own in her lap. More to herself than to Arden, she said, "I've been thinking a lot this weekend, about you and me. We used to have good times together when you were a little girl, but lately we're mostly getting on each other's nerves."

Arden waited. It seemed strange hearing Gran say this out loud.

"I confess," Gran continued, "that I was a little bit jealous when you and Jake became such pals just at the very time you were supposed to be becoming a young lady. Maybe I've been too anxious for you to get on with growing up."

Arden didn't want to hear it. With a feeling of hopelessness she flopped backward on the pillow and gazed up at the ceiling. "That happens anyway," she said grimly. "One day you wake up and you can't make believe anymore. Everything is real . . . and boring."

"That's true," Gran conceded. "But only for a while. It's a transition time. The best part about growing up is finding out what you can do and learning to do it well." She patted Arden's knee, which was under the covers. "Maybe singing will be that for you, who knows?"

She got up then, and Arden felt the bed jolt slightly as the springs uncoiled. "I'm going to bed now," Gran said.

Arden smiled and held out her arms. Gran bent and kissed her cheek, the way she used to do long ago. "Thanks," Arden said. "I'm sorry I've been such a sourpuss all these weeks."

"I've been as big a sourpuss as you," Gran said. "The pickle people could've used us in their ads."

"Right," said Arden. She felt light and almost happy. She straightened her leg so that her foot rested in the warm spot where Gran had sat.

CHAPTER TWENTY

"SO, HOW WAS IT?" HILL BUTTERED HIS TOAST AS THE TWO OF them breakfasted alone in the dining room. His tone was casual, but Arden sensed that it was a serious question. He had come in late last night, long after she was asleep, so he hadn't heard about the weekend.

"Fine," she said. "DorJo's just the same as ever."

Hill looked directly into her eyes. "Is Haverlee?"

"You know it's not," she said, giving him a wry smile. "Don't you remember how it was last summer, when *you* were wilderness wandering?"

He sat back, blinking. "Wilderness wandering? *I* don't remember wandering anywhere . . ."

"Big Dad said you were in between where you'd been and where you were going," she said. She felt important, being able to tell him this. "Haverlee wasn't the same when you went back, was it?"

"I don't know whether I appreciate you guys talking about

me behind my back," he said, but he was smiling. "Big Dad was right, though. I *was* in a strange land, sure enough."

"You aren't anymore, are you?"

The dimple in his cheek deepened. "No—for right now, I'm at home here. But how about you, Aardvark? Is it getting any better for you?"

She didn't answer right away. She was aware of Gran moving about the kitchen humming to herself. Dad had left for work, and Mom was upstairs dressing for a job interview.

"It's starting to be," she said carefully, not willing to make rash statements.

"I'm glad," Hill said simply. He wiped his mouth with his napkin and stood up. "If you'll get your things together within the next ten minutes, I'll take you to Brinks on my way to school."

In answer, she picked up her full glass of milk and drained it without stopping to breathe. Gran walked into the dining room just as she finished.

"Arden, for goodness' sake, it isn't healthy to gulp your milk down like that—or ladylike, either!"

"It is if I want a ride to school," Arden said, jumping up from the table. She gave Gran a swift kiss on the cheek. "See you this afternoon."

Gran's expression softened. Arden thought of the way Gran's eyes used to twinkle when Big Dad teased.

Riding to school in the VW beside Hill, she felt that something was different. Spring had arrived in a serious way, but she admitted to herself that the difference might have something to do with her own insides. It was very strange, going to school without dread.

Tyrone was there near the front entrance waiting for her.

"You sounded so scared about the duet I was afraid you'd chicken out and not come today," he said.

She made a face at him. "I *am* sort of scared . . . but excited, too. I guess I don't really believe it yet."

The bell clanged and the mass of students surged toward the building. Arden let herself be pushed through the doors and down the hall. For the first time since she came to Brinks, she didn't feel like shrinking from the press of bodies and the noise. She made her way upstairs to the locker, where she found Tiffany busily stuffing in an extra pair of shoes and a gym suit.

"Hey!" said Arden, smiling. "Did you leave me some room?"

"Yep," said Tiffany. She smiled back, a bit cautiously. It occurred to Arden that maybe Tiffany hadn't ever seen her really smile.

Arden took books from her pack and stuck them on the locker shelf. "No problem. This is all the space I need."

"Well . . . see you later," Tiffany called cheerfully, already on her way down the hall. Arden stood by the locker a moment longer. She began to remember the friendly person she used to be, the one who had been gone for so long.

In language arts, she sought out the girl named Hannah who had come up to her after she made her speech about Haverlee.

"What part of the coast are you from?" Arden asked her.

Hannah smiled shyly. "Not so far from Haverlee," she said. "I'm from Bear's Neck."

"We should've been comparing notes," Arden said. "How long have you lived here?"

"Two years."

"I just went back to visit Haverlee this weekend," Arden said, surprised at herself for saying these things to someone she scarcely knew. "I . . . think I'm about to get over being homesick."

Hannah nodded as though she understood. "I thought I'd

never stop missing Bear's Neck. I did, finally, but I still like to go back to visit. I'm glad I grew up there."

Her words echoed in Arden's head long after Miss Ferree had called the class to order and begun the day's lesson. *I'm glad I grew up there.* Haverlee really had been the best sort of place to grow up in.

That afternoon, Mr. Kale stopped her as soon as she walked through the door of the choral room. "I trust Tyrone told you about the duet," he said, without preliminary. He handed her a piece of sheet music. She stared, unbelieving. On the front were the words, Come Out the Wilderness. Her eyes filled as she flipped the page and saw the words of the song: "Tell me, how did you feel when you come out the wilderness . . . ?"

"What's wrong?" asked Mr. Kale, concerned.

She couldn't speak. She pointed to the title and shook her head. Mr. Kale would never understand, not in a million years.

"It's a well-known spiritual," he said, as though that should explain everything. "This is a new arrangement. It shouldn't be too difficult."

Tyrone came in just then. He pointed to a paper in his hand. "Social studies," he said. "Eighty on the last test."

"You better watch it, Tyrone—you'll be in the ninth grade next thing you know." Mr. Kale smiled. "Now—you two come over to the piano. I want to hear your voices together. Maybe I've just *imagined* this will work."

"But I never saw this music before now!" Arden protested. "I can't do it."

"Try," said Mr. Kale. "I'll play it through once." He sat down at the piano. Arden watched the notes, listened to the melody, tapped her foot. Beside her, Tyrone hummed his part softly.

"Now, I'll play the intro again and you just launch into it,"

Mr. Kale said. "Don't worry about mistakes. Keep going—okay?"

Arden began to sing, uncertainly at first. But Tyrone's pleasing harmony invited her to join in more strongly. She swayed with the rhythm, feeling the music's rocking beat all through her body. Before long, they were singing as though they had rehearsed for days.

They went through all the stanzas and refrains without stopping, ending together on a long, high third in perfect harmony. Applause broke out behind them like a sudden shower of rain. Whirling in surprise, Arden saw delight and amazement in the faces of her classmates as they clapped and cheered. She saw Tyrone's wide grin and Mr. Kale's satisfied smile. She heard her name shouted along with Tyrone's.

Suzanne Newton says, "In the beginning, the theme that chose me was loss—particularly the loss of moving from a beloved place and way of life to one that seems utterly strange. This is particularly hard for young people, and usually no one deals with that grief as real grief.

"In the actual writing of the book, however, some other themes emerged. One of them is the experience of being between places, that awkward and terrifying stage when you can't go back to where you were, but there isn't yet a place to which you can go. I call it 'Wilderness Wandering.' Grief itself is a kind of wilderness wandering, a process of letting go of the past in order to be fully in the present."

Ms. Newton grew up in Bath and Washington, North Carolina, towns somewhat like the fictional Haverlee in *An End to Perfect* and *A Place Between*. The mother of four grown children, she lives in Raleigh, where she works in the Poetry-in-the-Schools program and teaches creative writing at Meredith College.